Brenna Lyons

Monsters and Mayhem

FIREBORN
PUBLISHING

Fireborn Publishing Copyright Statement

PUBLISHER

FIREBORN
PUBLISHING

**PO Box 5216
Haverhill, MA 01835**

Tether

I will never understand how I drew this shit detail. I'd been a loyal employee of M.N.I.—Magical Needs, Inc.—for more than a decade. I'd never faulted in my assigned duties. They said that was why I was chosen for this transport, that I was the only woman they felt sure would be able to follow through.

I don't buy it for a second. I'm certain I lost a bet I don't remember making...or that they were sure I was the only person who wouldn't quit when faced with this transport. Maybe they were even counting on my feminine sensibilities to keep me from killing my little charge.

If that was what they were counting on, they were wildly mistaken. Ten days into my toughest transport yet, I could have gleefully killed the little twerp. I could have smiled and whistled while I did it and roasted marshmallows on his pyre.

In fact, I was probably fantasizing about it in that musty, rotting old barn somewhere in Colorado. The mental image had made the last few days of that almost two-week transfer bearable.

Your typical transport detail is a simple affair. You carry the item in a dampening box that, to the uninitiated, looks to be a briefcase or backpack. A masking spell makes it scan on x-ray and other devices as being full of file folders or gym socks...or whatever the magical geeks come up with to amuse themselves.

A third spell offers a mild compulsion to keep officials from opening it to check for themselves.

The spells aren't illegal. T.S.A. approved the base models decades ago. Not that they had much choice in the matter. M.E., Magical Enforcement, hadn't given them a choice in the matter. Between prejudice and avarice, keeping everyone but the transporter ignorant is always a good policy.

Even your average magical creature is intelligent and possessing of enough self-control to behave like a human when masked in human shape for a few hours or days. But not the one I was transporting. Damn the luck.

The crack of splitting wood and crash of it hitting the floor a dozen feet to my left rear wrung a sigh from me. After ten days, it had ceased to amaze or shock me.

"Damned gremlin."

"Gremlin has a name," the rusty, rasping voice came from behind me.

"Yes, Konrad. I know."

He pattered away, footsteps that would be unheard by anyone but me. In fact, though dampening and masking fields wouldn't work on Konrad, his nature made him imperceptible to anyone but the one holding his tether. For the trip to the buyer, that lucky individual was me.

Another beam creaked ominously, this one to the right rear, and I pushed to my feet. The mental checklist of things I couldn't do on this detail grew by one more. I couldn't seek shelter in an abandoned structure, unless I wanted to wake under the wreckage of it. Since that wasn't my first, second, or last choice of how to wake, it was off the menu.

Good thing it was summer, I guess. As long as the weather held a few more days, I'd survive it.

"Come on, Konrad. Let's go for a walk." Maybe we could make it to the next town and buy a sleeping bag and some fire blocks before nightfall.

Since gremlins attacked mechanical and electrical equipment, I knew that would be safe. I'd simply break the zipper before Konrad could do something to it. Broken things hold no appeal for gremlins. Fire blocks are chemical, and so are matches. It would be the perfect solution. I tried to convince myself of that, then gave up with a curse of disgust.

"Just one more, Allie," Konrad pleaded.

I looked over my shoulder, tracing the beam he was working on silently. It wasn't a main beam, and what it would drop was a section of roof opposite my position. "Sure. Knock yourself out." A bored gremlin was a bad thing. If dropping another beam would stave off the moment he decided he was "bored" again, it was worth a few minutes in the moldering barn.

The grinding metal that announced the bolts reaching their breaking points made me cringe. Konrad's leap from the beam to the ground behind me—a full ten-yard jump and twenty-foot drop—sent me backpedaling, and I tripped over him and landed on the floor. My skull cracked off the wood hard enough to make my head spin, but I knew Konrad would be fine. Gremlins are incredibly durable creatures.

Maybe killing him wouldn't have been as easy as I sometimes imagine it would have.

"Run, Allie. Run."

"Oh, shit." When a gremlin says to run, it's bad news. It had only taken me two days to learn that.

I scrambled to my feet and tore after him, stumbling when he reached the end of the tether and yanked my wrist out from my body mid-stride.

For probably the thousandth time since I met him, I wished I could shorten the tether. Usually, it was to keep him from getting into so much trouble. This time, it was to keep track of him in the dust clouds rising up.

Shifting overhead sent me into high gear. My mind numbly worked out that I'd been shortsighted in my decision to let him drop the beam. I hadn't been watching him, and with a gremlin, that was a bad idea. While I'd been focused on the single beam, I'd missed the fact that he'd loosened the bolts on them all. The entire barn was coming down around me.

Guess that's why I'm not an engineer.

The last thought to flit through my mind after the rafter cut into my forehead and sent me sprawling sideways onto the dust outside amounted to: *Oh, but gremlins are.*

Then blackness closed over me, and the roar of cracking timbers faded away.

* * * *

"Allie. Wake, Allie. I need something to play with." Konrad stood over me, looking annoyingly innocent and playful, without a hint of worry or confusion marring his expression.

If anyone else could see him, they'd probably think Konrad a fresh-faced preschooler, both in size and

4

appearance. Close inspection would reveal the elongated toes and fingers with heavy calluses that would grip on almost any surface from tree bark to smooth metal or fiberglass walls and the thick fingernails that acted as his many tools. But, at a distance, he looked like a chubby—nearly darling—child.

Darling. Yeah right. I started working my way to sitting, aching from head to toe.

Beside me, Konrad wiggled and moved from foot to foot, itching to be in motion to something...anything he could destroy, disassemble, or sabotage. "Play, Allie. I need something to *play* with."

Yes, he looked like a child. Even his clothing would put one in mind of a young boy in some remote place, playing barefoot in fields. His clothing had no fasteners, of course. What gremlin could resist breaking them? But his tunic and trousers fit just as his mother had created them when she was his age and had her children. According to the transport file, that would be about two-hundred and fifteen years old, young adult for a gremlin.

I blinked my eyes, considering his words. *Play. Of course!* All I had to do was get him some complex toys and simple electronics to keep him busy, and I could get him to the site outside Denver with a minimum of fuss. Why hadn't I thought of that earlier? Anything I bought to aid in the transport would be charged to the buyer anyway.

"Okay, Konrad. Let's get you something to play with."

Saying I was a little dizzy would be the understatement of the century. Worse, my hair was matted down with blood and the grit I'd picked up when Konrad had tried to drag my unconscious body.

Luckily, he'd dragged me the right way. Backtracking would have pissed me off.

The little twerp kept busy, helping me open the medical supplies and sanitary supplies I needed to walk into town and not get myself immediately arrested or carted off to the psych intervention unit. Since they were chemicals, Konrad had no innate interest in the med pack. Gremlins don't open boxes and scatter things. That's a trick for poltergeists or brownies. But tearing open the packets of IPA wipes and bandages gave him something to do besides walk along the deserted road with me.

Once that was done, Konrad raced ahead, taking apart road signs we passed. I thought about stopping him, but as I've already noted, there is nothing worse than a bored gremlin.

Besides that, since I wasn't carrying any tools—always a good idea when traveling with a gremlin—no one could blame me for the destruction of public property. If they suggested I did it, I'd have to point out that I could hardly remove bolts with my dirty fingernails, laughing to myself the whole time.

If the sign had warned of a hairpin turn, I probably would have stopped him. Probably. With my head aching and my mood so sour, I might not have. Someone else should be suffering with me, after all.

The town was called Liota, and it was probably named after some settler's wife. There wasn't much to it, but I knew an extended stay with a gremlin would flatten it, all the same.

After the first disastrous stop in a town, Konrad and I had come to an agreement. He could "play" in town as long as his play was nowhere near children and nowhere near me. Adults could fend for themselves, and if I was at the counter, and something happened at the far side of the store—say, a shelf fell—it clearly wasn't my fault, tools or not. Konrad had enough self-control to live by those two rules, which meant my sanity was marginally intact.

At that point in the trip, I was just glad I wasn't delivering him to the Deep South or the Ozarks, where some people still believed in jinxes and would run a suspected jinx out of town. Or worse, the local practitioners would try to press a warding of a non-existent curse or haunting on me. It was bad enough being tethered to a gremlin. The last thing I needed was sage and chicken feathers cooked over a black candle to top it.

That's why no employee wanted to handle a transport that couldn't be dampened. Magic that showed could complicate your transport in unexpected ways.

The first stop was the sporting goods store. It was first, because it was the first of the stops I needed that I came to on the main street through town. The last thing I wanted to have to do with a "curious as a basket full of kittens" gremlin was backtrack. West we were moving, and west we would continue to move.

I had the sleeping bag and fire blocks in short order. I passed by the tents with a shudder of revulsion. A knapsack—straps and not zippers or buckles—completed that purchase. Since nothing crashed or otherwise self-destructed while I was

7

shopping, I contented myself with hopes that people would find simple mechanical failures in some of the equipment bought there over the next week or month.

The toy store was next. My knapsack full of electronic toys and building toys, I took my leave to the incessant and blaring repetition of the first line of a Barney song from a stuffed toy. A young and very harried clerk tried desperately to get the batteries out of a jammed battery casing. I smiled weakly at that. At last, someone was sharing my misery, but while her misery was short-lived, mine would continue for several more days.

Making it this far had been a miracle of sorts. Any public transportation or private vehicle was out of the question. It wouldn't last two hours with Konrad on board, and whatever havoc ensued would likely kill his transporter in the process. Unless you are accomplished at riding a horse with no bridle and saddle, there is no way to travel that way, either. That meant walking. Walking for well over a week without benefit of a hotel or other comforts Konrad could knock down around my ears.

It was a good thing the bonus I was getting on this transport would pay for two weeks at a luxury resort in the islands. If my nerves and state of mind were any indication, I'd need it.

The final stop was Radio Shack. I loaded up on every type of small, cheap mechanical device I could find. If it seemed strange to the clerk, he kept it to himself and rang the order up without question.

I managed to convince Konrad not to break the snack and soda machines around the corner until I'd used them, and I bought an ice cream and burger on the way out of town at a walk-up window at Dairy Queen.

I was nearly out of town when the sheriff spotted me and pulled up beside me. He was courting trouble, though he didn't know it. A nice, shiny police car with the engine running was like candy to a gremlin, and sure enough, I saw Konrad duck under the front bumper to take a look.

"Just passing through?" the sheriff inquired from behind dark sunglass lenses.

"Yep. I'm doing an informal nature study for my classes, but it's a mite colder than I thought at night. I decided a sleeping bag was a good idea, so I stopped by to buy one." One thing a transporter for M.N.I. learns is to spin a tall tale to fit the occasion.

"And fire blocks, too."

Small towns are like that. It didn't surprise me that he knew what I'd bought. I nodded, because I figured he wanted an answer.

"Don't be starting a forest fire out there."

"No sir. I know all about fire restrictions and clearing a proper fire ring." I did, but it didn't hurt to say it.

"Toys and electronics are some funny things for someone doing a nature study to buy, don't you think?"

I feigned confusion. "Not really. The electronics give me something to do in my downtime, and I'll be stopping by to see some friends a few towns over. Just can't stop by and not bring the kids something, you know."

"A few towns over. Which town would that be?" He feigned interest as well as I did confusion, I noted.

The map of the area in one part of my mind and my calculation of how long it would be for the car to stop working in another, I smiled. "Kiowa."

He scanned me up and down, one cheek screwed up in a dubious look. "Looks like you've had a rough trip."

"Just slipped in some mud and took a header down a hill. You know cuts on the head. They bleed like hell, but they're nothing serious."

"Sure you don't need medical care?"

Just the thought of Konrad in some unsuspecting clinic or emergency room was enough to send chills down my spine. "Nah. It's disinfected. Nothing more a doctor is going to do."

"I don't know about letting someone with a head injury wander around. Want a ride?" he offered.

To speed me out of town and make sure I leave. "No thanks. They aren't expecting me for two days, and I have some more surveys to take on the peak tomorrow. If I start walking now, I'll be right where I need to be on time."

"Are you–"

Right on schedule, the car sputtered and died.

"What the hell?" The sheriff tried to start it, but the starter churning was the only sound the abused vehicle made. "I just got this tuned up last week," he complained.

"If you don't mind, Sheriff... I really need to get moving."

He glared at me, then waved me along.

A block away, the crowd starting to gather to help the lawman, I let my smile break free. "Nothing that will look too suspicious, I hope, Konrad?" I whispered.

10

The gremlin skipped along beside me, carrying a frayed chunk of wire that looked suspiciously like it belonged on a distributor cap. "No, Allie. I was just playing."

* * * *

While Liota's sheriff was probably searching for me in Kiowa, I was a few towns north and a few miles east, on the outskirts of Bennett. Since I wasn't really doing surveys, I could travel a lot faster than the sheriff would give me credit for.

The building toys had kept Konrad busy for a few hours, at best. I'd built increasingly complex, moving designs and let him take them apart. But, a gremlin is smarter than that and learns quickly. Though he looked like a four-year-old, his mind was much more complex. By the end of the day when I left Liota, he'd gone through three of the electronic toys and was begging me for a fourth.

The last few toys and the first two of the handheld electronics got us through the next day, supplemented by a few hapless road signs that we happened upon in the "I'm bored" hour or so I'd make him wait before giving him another machine to strip down, rewire, or otherwise destroy.

I'd been rationing out the rest over the last day. By my estimation, he'd be "bored" again right about the time I handed him over to his buyer. The thought of that put a spring in my step.

Disbelief stopped me in my tracks on the access road. I pulled the map and double-checked it against the directions my boss had given me in the middle of a field outside Goodland, Kansas. Certain I'd started hallucinating, I checked them again.

No. They matched. The damned fool was having me hand Konrad over at his own factory. That was the stupidest idea I'd ever heard of. Gremlins were typically passed hand to hand in wide open spaces with no machines to attract the little guys.

What the buyer did after that was his own business. Usually, it amounted to having a spy set up in manufacturing or maintenance with a competitor take the gremlin in and tether him in the warehouse, garage, or assembly shop—causing a completely untraceable series of disasters, broken equipment, and fouled product. Only a fool would bring a gremlin into his own factory and risk what could happen next.

Oh well, he's *the fool then.* I didn't doubt that Steve, my boss, had tried to talk the buyer out of this, but in the end, M.N.I. is just a transport company. We deliver where the buyer wants the goods delivered.

Who knows? Maybe he wants Konrad to destroy his own factory for the insurance money. If he did, it was none of my business. I'm just the delivery person, after all. Whatever happens after I make delivery is out of my hands. If a buyer uses the magic illegally, it's on his head and not mine.

The less I know, the better. Confidentiality is a Magical Needs, Inc. staple. That's why we get seventy-five percent of all magical transport calls. We don't ask. We don't tell. We don't want to know. Short of transporting an illegal magical item or creature, the company keeps its collective nose out of the buyer's business.

I made sure Konrad had a fresh calculator before I approached the guard shack. Still, he glanced up at the narrow door to the shack, his eyes shining.

Telling him to stand down would be a bad move. For one thing, the guard wasn't supposed to know what I was delivering, and talking to something invisible indicated some magical creature. Or it indicated you were crazy. Either way, it wasn't ideal to let the guard see me talking to thin air.

Process me through quickly, and you won't have to explain something broken in your shack.

The guard scowled at me. "Can I help you, miss?"

"Miz," I corrected him. "Barnes. And, I'm here to see Mr. George Warrington Ellis The Younger. He's expecting me. Mr. Shottenhower sent me with a package for him."

Steve's last name wasn't Shottenhower any more than mine was Barnes, but the mantra of "the less they know, the better" worked both ways. For our own protection, there were things the buyers didn't need to know.

The guard picked up the phone, and Konrad's eyes started to gleam in a way that told me time was running out. There were prettier toys to play with than the one I'd given the gremlin.

"Looks like you had a rough trip." The guard started punching in the code he needed.

"Heavy rains. The car went off the road in the mud this morning."

His grunt of agreement said I'd gotten past that hurdle. It never ceased to amaze me that I could give a similar story in the middle of a desert that almost never saw rain and have people agree that mud from a storm was a bad thing and congratulate me on surviving it.

"Well, good thing you got out with so little damage."

Predictable. "Yeah. It was." Konrad certainly hadn't made it easy on me.

"Mr. Ellis doesn't like to be kept waiting."

"Believe me, I will be glad to hand this over and get to a hotel to clean up."

He didn't answer that. "Charlotte, there's a delivery here for Mr. Ellis from a Mr. Shottenhower. Should I send the courier up?"

There was a moment of silence.

"Right away." The guard hung up and turned to me, interest I didn't need sparkling in his eyes. "Can we give you a lift to the factory, Ms. Barnes?" He reached for the phone again.

A small hand came up behind him, and I saw screws backing out of the phone housing behind a thick fingernail. The urge to laugh built up in me, and I turned it to a bright smile. "No thank you. Maybe as I'm leaving. I'm not looking forward to getting in a car again so soon." *With Konrad still tethered to me, that is.*

"Yes, Ma'am. The office entrance is to the left of the building, and Mr. Ellis's office is on the top floor."

"Thanks very much."

I headed up the access road and toward my moment of freedom. Konrad was apparently engrossed in his "play," and the tether bit into my wrist for a moment before he followed along. Without missing a beat, I handed off a pedometer to Konrad to keep him occupied. It had to be something new to occupy him.

After two calculators of different types, it was a certain thing that a third would bore him.

"Nothing worse than a bored gremlin. Right, Konrad?" I muttered.

"You said it," he piped up. As always, his voice was incongruous to his looks. He had the voice of a sixty-year-old smoker and the face of a cherub.

And the sense of humor of a young demon. I would know. I'd transported a few lightly dampened demons in my time. In the last thirteen days, I'd decided that I'd take on an undampened demon before I took on another gremlin for longer than a day.

Convincing Konrad up the stairs to the office wasn't the easiest thing in the world. One peek through the open double doors to the factory floor and it was like dragging a flailing Kindergartener away from Disneyland.

Finally, he came with me, though he did so stomping his feet in a way that made my damaged head ache all the worse. Over and over again, I promised him that his new owner would let him play to his heart's content. No one purchased a gremlin without some mischief the gremlin would love in mind.

Ellis's secretary didn't keep me waiting. She vaulted from behind her polished mahogany desk and opened the inner door for me the moment I stepped through the outer one.

I'd like to think she did it because she knew how important the delivery was, but the truth was she was probably unnerved by my appearance and smell. Sanitary wipes can only do so much toward keeping a person sanitary, and I was in desperate need of a long soak in a hot tub.

Ellis wasn't as quick to address the issue. Five minutes after the door closed behind me and the last two small contraptions to Konrad later, he was still staring at a blueprint on his desk. Annoyed, I cleared my throat.

He looked up, scowling at me. "Ah, yes. I trust you have the delivery with you?" His voice was nasally and unpleasant.

"The delivery is taking a marked interest in your bookshelves." He wasn't, but I figured that would bring the risk Ellis was taking home to him, and the bookshelves looked to be hand-made mahogany and not something he'd want in splinters. "You might want to get Konrad to someplace where it's safe for him to cause some havoc."

"Konrad?"

"The gremlin's name is Konrad. He gets a little testy, if you don't use it."

He didn't look impressed. "I was led to believe that gremlins were unintelligent creatures."

"Too intelligent and inquisitive for their own good is more like it...or ours," I corrected him.

"How good is it?"

My cheeks burned in indignation. Konrad wasn't a thing. "He destroyed the test facility in fourteen days. That is—"

"Five days faster than the norm and only two days shorter than the record. Acceptable."

"Did Mr. Shottenhower explain that Konrad is—"

"On a tether." His tone was clipped and cold.

"Well, yes, but—"

"Please, give me the tether, Ms. Barnes."

His dismissal floored me. Didn't he understand the chance he was taking here?

Maybe he does want to cash in on the insurance money. Stranger things had happened in my life, after all. This one wasn't even unusual.

Or maybe he wants to "discover" the gremlin and accuse his competitor of planting Konrad. No. If he wanted that, he wouldn't have met the little creature at all. On questioning, Konrad would know who his tether holders had been.

"Ms. Barnes?"

Whatever his plan, it was on his head. I'd done my job and delivered Konrad to his rightful owner. The laws for magical transporters stated that, as long as I didn't deliver illegal goods—and I hadn't—any fallout was the responsibility of the purchaser.

Resolved, I loosened the magical tether and reached for his wrist. "You'll want to keep track of him, Mr. Ellis. And make sure he has something you approve of to play with. There's nothing worse than a bored gremlin."

"But he's tethered."

"Did anyone tell you how long the–"

"Just give me the damned tether."

"Yes, sir." I secured Konrad to his arm, pulled out the shipping order, and got Ellis's signature.

"Doesn't look like much, does he?" Ellis scowled deeply, staring at what was probably Konrad, though I couldn't see him anymore to be certain.

"I think Konrad is rather sweet, once you know how to handle him." *Last chance to find out the easy way.*

"If that will be all?" he hinted.

"I was told you would provide a ride for me into town. I walked the distance, after all."

"Ah...yes. Slipped my mind. Charlotte will give you the keys to one of the cars. Leave it at the rental car lot when you pick up your car to the airport in Denver."

"Thank you, sir. And please keep M.N.I. in mind for any further transportation needs." Even injured and tired, any employee could deliver that line with a straight face. I could do it better than most. Good thing, too. Telling Ellis I'd welcome another job for him was a bald-faced lie.

Ten minutes later, I was past the guard house and on my way to Denver. An hour later, I was safely in a rental car and on my way to Wyoming, Idaho, and Oregon beyond.

Ellis didn't need to know where I was headed. On more than one occasion, I'd found that the less the buyer knew about me, the better it was. Ellis struck me as the sort that I didn't want knowing too much about me.

* * * *

I stepped out of the shower and onto the plush bathmat on the floor of the Regency bathroom. In the bedroom, the television blared.

Until I was out of the area of a job, I always kept an ear open for some magic-based mishap that might have befallen the new owner. As Steve often said, very few people had the proper respect for the magic they thought they wanted.

This time, I was more anxious than most. It was a slow simmer low in my gut that warned Ellis would do

18

something stupid, either to me or accidentally with Konrad. Dealing with magic, you learn to trust your gut.

I'd changed cars in Salt Lake City and taken a low-end motel room there to knock off the worst of the road dust and get some new clothes. In Portland, I'd started stocking up for my trip to the islands, but first I'd planned a two-day layover to recoup. The Regency offered everything I'd need: saunas and hot tubs, a five-star restaurant, massages, and nearby stores to do a little relaxing in.

Dressed and fluffed, I reached for my purse, but the television brought me up short.

"George Warrington Ellis died today in a partial collapse of his factory complex outside Denver. Local authorities have yet to explain the unequal fraying of the overhead support lines on one side of the massive structure. Early examinations have ruled out tampering. The tentative explanation is settling of one corner of the building, leading to stress on that corner."

I didn't look at the screen. I didn't have to. I could imagine that the factory looked much like a certain barn I'd visited recently did.

Mapping out the fifty yards the tether gave Konrad brought a smile to my face. Obviously, Mr. Ellis thought he'd been safe enough keeping the gremlin in his office, far from the production floor. By not listening to my warning about how long the tether was, he hadn't realized what else Konrad could reach.

"And he didn't watch you. Less than two days. Good job, Konrad." He'd officially broken the record. "And Mr. E said you didn't look like much." It should have galled me that I was proud of the little twerp, but it didn't.

The television turned off, I ambled out of the hotel and toward a shop I'd decided to visit before I left the states. The new cell phone I'd purchased in Salt Lake in hand, I called Steve.

"Mr. Scott, please?" I informed the computer routing system.

He answered on the first ring. "Ms. Allie Billings," he crowed. "My favorite transporter. Great job with the delivery."

"You've seen the latest news?" There was no time to pull punches.

There was a clicking of computer keys on the other end of the line. "So sad. I assume I'll need to call the authorities." He sighed.

"Better you than me, Steve."

"What's the situation?"

Magical Enforcement would need to know there was a gremlin that might be without an active human tether, so they could collect him and return him to a safe facility. An unsecured magical creature or item is the only reason we interfere in a buyer's business, after the fact. That is the law.

"Last I saw, Konrad was tethered to him, but he could have tethered him to anything in the office. Or, he could have handed Konrad over to a third party before the collapse. That means we don't know for certain where Konrad is now, but we can't chance that he's on a dead tether."

Steve swore fluently.

"I tried to warn him how long the tether is, but he wasn't listening." It couldn't hurt to remind him of that.

"Typical. People never have the proper respect for handling dangerous equipment or creatures." There was a moment of silence. "You know, M.E. is going to request a transport. It's good money, Allie."

"For someone else. I was promised a couple of weeks in paradise."

"Aw, Allie–"

I smiled against the handset. "Time for someone else to share my misery." For once, I didn't care if it was Steve himself. "Besides that, I'm a delivery person. I don't take returns. Not my department."

Welcome To Hell

"Home," Sharon Sullus repeated, putting the steel in her voice that typically sent her employees scattering. "Take me home, *now*."

The mocking smile curving his lips preceded a laugh that taunted her, challenged her, called her a child. "It's simple enough–"

"You're asking me to commit a murder." She pinched herself, praying this was some demented dream, wincing at the slice of pain in her upper arm. "Too much to ask," she muttered.

"For the last time, Sherri–"

"Sharon," she snapped, her nerves crackling in exhaustion and irritation. She'd always hated that nickname, and no one had used it since her aunt died.

His smile widened, and he stretched out on the soaking grass, crossing his legs at the ankles. "It's simple, *Sharon*. We're in the past. You don't exist here. How can you commit a murder in a time you don't exist?"

Sharon pressed her hands to her aching head. "I *do* exist. I'm standing right here in my favorite PJs, my socks soaking wet and filthy...and freezing to boot." *Late April and no coat.* She supposed it could be worse; the "how" was illusive.

She glared at him, noting his continued amusement in frustration. "If I commit a murder here, I commit a murder." *By definition, a murder means someone or something is killed.* That was not an option plan.

He sighed. "It won't be a—"

"Is someone going to be dead?" she countered icily. "I—would—be—killing—someone." Just the thought of it churned her stomach, and she started pacing, her arms crossed over her belly, wishing for some of the Tums Ultra stored in her medicine cabinet.

"You'll be stopping her from killing someone else. You'll be executing a murderess and saving an innocent man."

She turned on him. "Then why don't you do it, Sam Beckett? You're supposed to be the almighty time lord, aren't you?"

"Time hopper," he corrected.

"What-*ever*. This is your problem, not mine. You take care of it."

He rose from the ground, unfurling like flower in the sun...or a snake. Despite her better judgment, Sharon had to admit he was a good-looking man, possessing of an animal grace, a nearly-feral, prowling presence that made her heart pound in something other than fear and anger.

Then he was face-to-face with her, his head cocked to one side, starkly serious. "I cannot interfere in anything that intersects my own...timeline."

Her breath came in shallow gasps. "Why me?" she managed.

His hand rose, hovering a whisper from her cheek. He didn't make contact. Instead, he stared at her. "You're perfect," he breathed. "Perfect."

Sharon shook her head in confusion, dimly noting his hand moving away. Why did nothing he say make sense to her?

"I have watched you all your life, Sharon. I was there when you were born...in the prison infirmary. They didn't make it to the county hospital like your birth certificate says."

He can't know that.

"I was there when you achieved all of your firsts in life. Your first step, first word, first...kiss. When you laughed...and when you cried. This is your moment, Sharon. This is your destiny. Do this..."

His hesitation made her heart pound faster, an alarming cadence.

"And I will take you back."

Some sane corner of her mind argued that Sharon should be frightened by this entire thing, chilled and appalled by the idea of him stalking her through time. Strangely, the thought was warming.

"Will you listen to what I have to say?" he asked.

Words came slowly, nearly in a daze. "What is your name?"

"Ayden. Ayden Blake."

"Well then, Ayden...I suppose I should at least hear you out."

His smile made her heart flutter excitedly. Ayden reached down and took her hand, threading his fingers through hers. Together, they turned toward the tree line.

Sharon paused, a shiver working down her spine. Someone might describe the meadow they were standing in as idyllic. Even Sharon might have said it, under other circumstances.

But the skyline towering over the tree line, a cameo in the setting sun, was all too familiar. It was the skyline she saw every night from her bedroom window, peering over the peaks of rooftops lower on the hill.

Those rooftops didn't exist in this time. Her house—a three-bedroom, two-bath, split-level, loosely based on an old Frank Lloyd Wright design—had never been. Her feet sank into a soft mat of grass where her garage had once rested.

Will rest, she reminded herself. *Someday, in the future, it will rest here.* "When?"

Ayden turned to her, seemingly concerned. "When what, Sharon?"

"My house. That development was built twenty years ago–"

"Twenty-three," he corrected gently.

She nodded. "When... This sounds so demented."

He smiled. "Not to me."

"Right. When are we?"

"Nineteen-seventy-six."

Vertigo assaulted her, and Ayden caught her against his broad chest.

"Sharon?"

She gulped in air, fighting down her rising gorge. "I really don't exist here." It was a year before she was born.

* * * *

"Feeling better?" Ayden asked, his hand massaging at the back of her neck.

Sharon groaned, pressing the ice pack against her forehead. "Where did you get this?"

25

At his chuckle, she forced her eyes open. Ayden stared down at her, his dark eyes crinkled and edged in laugh lines.

"Wha–?" She sat forward, unfolding the towel full of ice on her lap with a shiver. Her signature double S monogram stared back at her.

Tears pricked at her eyes. "You went back without me." Just when she'd started to trust him, he played another mind game on her.

Ayden sighed. "Forward. Movement through time is complex."

"I'll bet," she drawled.

"You are out of your natural time," he explained patiently. "Until–"

"Which you did to me!"

He winced. "It's complex."

"So you keep saying."

"It will make sense soon. I promise it will, but we're running out of time."

Sharon laughed harshly, her logical mind fraying at the concept. "Time? A time hopper is running out of time?"

"You are not really a time hopper, Sharon. You can run out of time."

His expression was grim enough to cause her heart to stutter in response. Sweat slicked her body, making her shiver in the cool, evening wind. "What happens if I run out of time?"

For a long moment, he didn't answer. "Time is wrong, Sharon. We're here to patch a tear." He'd said that before. "Can't you feel the poison?"

She didn't want to admit it, but she could feel it. There was a sickly-sweet scent carried on the breeze.

Something black and oily oozed beneath the soil, just out of sight and reach, but close enough to strike at her.

"You feel it," he whispered. "I knew you would."

"Yes. I feel it."

"If this continues, everything in the time stream will be tainted."

"If I fail, can I go back?"

Ayden stared at her in apparent misery. "I don't know, Sharon. I really don't."

"But...if I do..."

"It will all be wrong," he confirmed for her.

She let that thought sink in. Did she want to return to a world poisoned by the muck she felt lurking beneath the topsoil? "What am I supposed to do? I mean *precisely* what."

The .32 appeared from the back of his jeans, probably hidden beneath the hooded sweatshirt he wore.

"No. There has to be another way. Not a gun." She couldn't use a gun. It went against everything her aunt had taught her, against everything Sharon believed.

"You are not your mother," he soothed her.

"What would you know?" she snapped.

One dark brow arched up.

Okay. So, he knows. "She was a murdering bitch, Ayden." *I will not become what she was.*

His features softened. "If that's true, so is this woman."

Sharon took a moment to digest that. Her life had been hell. Her aunt's life had been. And her parents—It was almost kinder not to think about their lives and ends.

"Watch," he instructed. "Listen. She will shoot him. Don't doubt it. The choice...ultimately, is yours."

Words stuck in her throat, and she swallowed a dry lump. "I'll look. I'll listen. Beyond that... No promises."

Ayden nodded his agreement. "Fair enough."

He also offered the handgun again. Sharon fisted her hands in her monogrammed towel, refusing to touch it. Ayden didn't persist; it disappeared into the back of his jeans.

* * * *

"If you don't like it, you're free to leave, baby," the man dismissed the woman he was conversing with.

Sharon squinted her eyes in the darkness, wishing the clouds would part and the moon light the scene for her. As it was, outlines and cameos were all she could make out between the trees.

"I didn't say–" the woman pleaded.

"Go back to your daddy and his blood money, if that's what you want."

"What a jerk," Sharon breathed. Was he really a loss?

Ayden's lips nestled to her ear. "Don't judge him too harshly. After all, she's a murdering bitch." It wasn't a taunt. It was a statement of fact.

But his comment made her miss whatever the woman replied to the jerk.

"She's breaking his heart, too," Ayden confided.

"Make your choice, baby. Just make your choice." He turned to leave.

And the gun came up in the bitch's hands.

The clouds parted, and moonlight highlighted the man's face. His light blue eyes sought out Sharon's, and her heart took up a non-rhythm. She knew that face. She knew those eyes, the eyes she'd inherited from him, eyes she'd only seen pictures of, until today. It was her father, John Sullus. There was no mistaking it.

Rational thought deserted her. Twice? He'd been shot by a woman he'd been intimate with twice? Did he think it couldn't possibly happen again? Was that what went wrong the second time?

Was that why Ayden didn't know if Sharon could go back if she failed? Because John Adam Sullus wouldn't be alive to be the genetic donor to her?

"Sully," the woman behind him screeched.

The woman holding the gun!

He turned, seemingly stunned.

The hand holding the weapon shook, the only clear part of her Sharon could see, thanks to the deep shadows beneath the trees.

"No," Sharon breathed. How many times had she asked herself what she'd do if she could meet her father? If she could save him? The question had been whispered to her in the night, over and over, until she thought she'd go mad thinking about it.

Ayden took her hand and turned it palm-up. The wood grip was a cool comfort, and Sharon wrapped her hand around it, bringing it to bear on the threat to her father. She fervently hoped it was ready to fire; Sharon certainly didn't know how to cock it or prime it or whatever it was called.

The weapon kicked back, sending shards of pain up Sharon's arm, knocking her back to rational thought just in time for all hell to break loose.

Her father vaulted toward the other woman with a wordless roar of pain. For a moment, Sharon was certain he'd been shot, as well. She'd failed.

Then his words reached her.

"No. No, you can't—there's so much blood."

Guilt mixed with jealousy coursed through Sharon.

The guilt was easy enough to categorize but not what she would have expected. She felt a certain amount of guilt over her complete lack of shame and remorse in shooting the woman. The lion's share of the dark emotion, though, stemmed from another source.

He'd obviously loved the woman, and losing her hurt him. John was the father she'd never met, and the last thing Sharon wanted was to cause him pain.

The jealousy, in a moment of crystal clarity, was even easier to lay claim to. This was likely the only chance they'd ever have, and he wanted to waste it mourning a murderess.

"Mary," he choked. "I know you wouldn't have hurt me."

Sharon rolled her eyes. *Yeah, right. She was going to—*

Mary! Realization hit hard. "No." It wasn't possible, was it?

It's spring, she rationalized. *I wasn't conceived until late summer. It can't be the same Mary.*

Her rational mind was less forgiving in making that determination. *Two women named Mary tried—*

Sharon shied from a damp flutter against her cheek. She raised her left hand, snagging the offending object from her shirt. It was a leaf, golden with edges of what she was abruptly certain was red.

It's spring. Just the thought of alternatives made her numb to the cold coursing through her veins.

Her stomach lurched at the thought of time hopping. *It was spring when I left. If I moved years, why not seasons? Ayden never said it was still spring. I never asked. It hadn't seemed important.*

Oh, but it was important. Wasn't it?

Her heart skittered, and her head spun sickly. The handgun slipped from her boneless fingers and thudded dully on the forest floor. Her wet, chilled feet carried her forward, but she felt nothing, as if they'd turned to ice beneath her.

The scant moonlight filtering through the trees illuminated the woman's pale face, making the drops of blood seem all the darker. Her eyes were wide and unfocused, her body trembling and jerking with each labored breath. Even in the shadows cast by tree branches, her red hair glowed.

My red hair. Though there'd conspicuously been no pictures of her mother allowed in her aunt's home, there was little question who this woman was.

Sharon pressed both hands to her mouth, shaking her head in disbelief. *They'll both live, now. They have to, or I won't exist.*

As if in answer, Mary Ellen Richards let out a thin breath and went still.

At first, Sharon was certain the feeling of separation was dizziness, the disconcerted feeling before a faint. Or maybe it was her mind fracturing under the stress of what she'd just done, the horrible choice she'd made.

In the next instant, her insubstantial state smacked solidly home. A peel of hysterical laughter escaped her lips as the pun occurred to her.

Her father turned, their gazes locking. His fury melted into a look of horror. Sharon reached for him...

She stumbled forward, landing on her knees. Smooth stone warmed her, but she shivered on. It was smooth as polished marble, hard as steel.

Bright sunlight stung her eyes after well over an hour of darkness. Sharon blinked, winced, forced a now-corporeal hand up with the expectation of looking through it as she had the moment before she fell through time again.

Her surroundings took shape slowly from the mists of her abused eyes. The white marble, columned building was set on rolling hills of grass, lightly waving in a gentle breeze. She knelt on a patio of the same marble that composed the attached building, uniform in color and unpitted by the ravages of time.

"Back," she managed numbly. "You promised to take me back."

Ayden didn't answer, though he started to circle her body.

Her mind hacked away at their conversations. "Forward. Home is forward. You said..." Sharon swiveled her head, looking for anything familiar...the skyline, the tree line. There was nothing of comfort here. "How far back? Where are we?"

He crouched before her, his expression unreadable. "What would you return to, Sharon? You don't exist there. You never have. Your former house belongs to a young couple expecting their first baby. It's a boy. His name is Aaron. Your former possessions were never sold to you. You are not even corporeal in that realm.

"Your mother died in early pregnancy. Your father went on to–"

"No!" She didn't want to hear this. If he married and had other children, children that had the chance to know him, she didn't want to know it. It was hard enough grasping that she'd killed herself in the womb. "You made me commit suicide. Why?" Why would he do that?

"I made you do nothing. You chose to repair the breach."

Sharon met his eyes, stunned by the compassion she saw. "What breach?"

"The gods write the story. Along the way, one of them gave the players...the humans the ability to write a small bit, as well."

"You mean free will." She settled on the stone, crossing her legs Indian-style.

Ayden did the same. "That's what they call it. It's really just people acting out of character. Amusing when you see the whole thing as a play and take Shakespeare's quote literally.

"John said he knew Mary never would have hurt him. As the gods wrote it...initially, she never would have."

"Initially?"

He shifted, as if discomfited by something. "The gods are a jealous bunch. You cross them, and they do terrible things."

"Like?" Sharon queried, though she wasn't entirely certain she wanted to know the answer to it.

"Like rewriting a story a character refuses to act in character in to show that character dead stage right."

Sharon closed her eyes, reeling at the thought of it. "So the original plan was?"

"The story, as written initially, was that they worked it out and had a life together with you. Not the happiest of lives, but life nonetheless."

She couldn't find the words to answer that.

"You see? They call it freewill, but there's nothing free about it."

"They call it? The gods, you mean?"

"Humans."

Sharon opened her eyes. "I'm human." It came out hollow. She suspected what his answer would be, and though she didn't want to face that unpleasant possibility, she had to hear it.

He shook his head, a slow, graceful series of hypnotizing arcs. "When you patched the tear between the play as written and as performed, you ceased to be human. Not all breaches involve unborns. Very few, in fact. Most are smaller tears, less obvious changes in the script."

"Am I dead? Is this...some sort of heaven, where I'll be reunited with my parents and aunt?" It was too beautiful to be hell.

Ayden sighed. "There is so much to explain, so many twists to dealing with time. It's so..."

"Complex," she offered his complaint of earlier.

"Yes. It is. You cannot be reunited with your parents and aunt, because you don't exist to them."

She nodded, her mood dipping further.

"Heaven is for humans and angels and gods. We are...other. Rather than consign us to the abyss, the gods made us this paradise to inhabit. After all, we were useful in righting their performance and sacrificing ourselves to their plans." There was a bite of something bitter and unforgiving in his voice.

"Take me ba... I mean, take me forward," she requested.

He cocked his head to one side, as if he didn't understand her.

"My former time," she managed shakily.

"Why would you want to see that?"

Explaining it rationally was impossible. It wasn't rational.

"Your existence is wrong, a breach in the gods' plan. It–"

"Who says the gods are right?" She fumed at that. Sharon had never cared much for gods, but she'd never believed they had something against her personally until this moment. It was rather galling, when you considered it.

A smile lit Ayden's eyes. "Now you're asking time hopper questions. In short, they are the most powerful, the top of the food chain. *They* say they're right, and you can't fight them."

"Watch me." She'd never backed down from a fight in her life. Not when she believed in what she was fighting for.

His smile turned sad. "You can't fight what you can't reach. I've tried."

"So...what? We hang around here until we die?"

"Sharon, you're not human. We're not. We're not a part of the gods' time stream. We don't age. We don't die. We just...are, because we were accidentally created and–"

"Story of my life," she snapped. Her heart ached. Sharon had always been an accident—an accident of her father's impetuous nature, her mother's miscalculation, dropped in her aunt's lap to raise. "Did they all have a better life without me?" she asked bitterly. Her aunt surely had.

"Some of them. Your father and aunt did. Others didn't. It's always a tradeoff."

She nodded. "I can...hop time then? If I'm like you, then I should be able to."

Ayden was silent for a long moment. "I'll teach you."

"Now?" At least, it would give her something to focus on, something to work toward and accomplish, now that her other goals and dreams had been stripped away with her "poisoned world."

"When you're not a danger to yourself." It was a simple, uncompromising statement.

"I don't understand that. If I can't die, how can I endanger myself?"

He sighed. "Where is the first place you'd go, Sharon?"

Her head spun. A hundred possibilities occurred to her at once. She could go anywhere, any time, see anything she wished. But where first?

"You think you know, but you'd choose to play the backward *It's a Wonderful Life* tour from hell. You have to be prepared to see that some people are better without you. It's one thing to hear it. It's another to see it, to be faced with a vision you can never shed."

"Did you make that mistake?"

His jaw tightened, and he offered a single, tense nod in response.

"And?" How bad could it be?

"It nearly destroyed my spirit to see it. When it's all you have left... It's the closest we have to hell here. Even the abyss would be preferable to a broken soul, hurting and without solace."

Sharon considered that. "I don't think I can live this way."

Ayden hesitated. "There is one true solace offered to us," he hedged. "One joy in this place."

She waited, barely breathing.

Am I breathing? She was going through the motions, but if she wasn't alive, was it breathing? There were a thousand questions and few answers. *But all the time in the universe to get those answers.* She understood a bit of Ayden's bitterness now.

"When we find another time hopper, we are permitted companionship...and passion."

All the looks and touches since she'd met him warred in her mind. "It's always been about that for you. That's why you said the outcome affected your timeline."

He didn't deny it. Nor did he appear apologetic.

Sharon launched at him in a rush of fury and hurt. In a blur of motion, Ayden had her under him, her wrists trapped in hands and his body pressing down on hers.

Her body reacted intensely to the connection, her nipples beading, breath going ragged, her body slicking to invite the cock rising against her thigh. She trembled in a mixture of need and revulsion at what she wanted from him.

Ayden's breath fanned over her lips, reinforcing how much more sensitive she was to touch in this non-state of being. Or was that a delusion? The mad urge to kiss him and test it wrestled with her outrage.

"We're going to be so good together," he rasped.

Sharon swallowed down acceptance. He did this without her permission. Ayden had tricked her. "Not in a hundred years," she vowed.

An edge of ice appeared in his eyes, giving them the appearance of obsidian—hard and inflexible. He pushed away from her, his gaze trailing down her body.

That simply, her arousal kicked up another notch.

"Possibly," he conceded. "A hundred years. A thousand. You're pretty angry, after all. But what is time to someone timeless?"

Ayden straightened his clothing. "When you're tired of being alone and want to spend time with me, call me. I'll hear you."

Before she could question him, Ayden was gone. Sharon lay there for a while, aching for what she'd refused him.

Finally she sat up and looked around again. Minutes, hours, days...perhaps centuries later, she realized that nothing changed here. The sun, if it was a star in an actual sky, never moved. There would be no day and night to pass time with.

There was a light but constant breeze that rustled the grass. That grass reached to the horizon. Sharon suspected that, if she walked for an eternity in any direction at random, she'd find nothing but the same endless, waving grass.

There were no people to talk to, no birds or other animals to add sound and texture to the pabulum around her. The whisper of the wind didn't even rightly qualify as white noise, because it never varied. There were no natural gusts and lulls. The gods had obviously not taken care to make this place three-dimensional.

It was a given that there was no music or other entertainment inside the structure. That would give her a sense of time—three minutes for a song, an hour for a television show, two hours for a movie...

"I was wrong," Sharon breathed. "This is hell."

#

Vlad stood in the shadows, watching the man across the town square, his brother...and his greatest enemy. How had it all gone so wrong?

Abraham had been a happy child. Father's second wife, Vlad's mother, had taken Abraham under her wing, suckled him at her breast, and treated him with a fondness to match her own children and the respect due Father's eldest son. Abraham had always been content with his life. Until he reached the age of ten and six; until he was a man. With adulthood came the hunger and the truth of Abraham's existence.

Vlad sighed. It was their father's fault. Drac should have told Abraham that he must remain as he was, that he could never have his fondest wish—never claim his birthright. Their father had cowered, pretending the day of conflict would never come, but come it had.

Vlad had never seen Abraham so angry. His elder brother had shouted, destroyed everything in his path, sent his younger siblings scattering as he demanded his birthright as first son. Still, Drac had denied him, pleading understanding for the vow he'd made to his first wife, the vow that stole Abraham's birthright, the vow that stole the gift of immortality from him that she herself had refused even as she lay dying from childbirth gone wrong. Drac had loved her dearly. As such, nothing could move him to relinquish that vow, not even the loss of the son he'd wronged.

Abraham left that very night, sparing not even a glance for Vlad, the new heir and yet the only one of the younger sons who would have gifted Abraham his birthright that night if he were able to do such a thing. Vlad would have sought Abraham out the moment he was gifted to pass the gift along were it not for their father's blood link preventing him from doing it.

Drac had openly grieved the loss of his eldest son, his last link to the first woman who captured his heart in his long and gruesome lifetime. Vlad suspected their father had also sighed in relief that he no longer carried the hateful secret in his heart, no longer faced the confrontation he'd dreaded for ten and six long years.

That was what Vlad had come to expect of Drac. It had been a chore for Vlad, pretending to respect the Lord of All, a man who had ceased to live when his first wife died, who was so weary of confrontation that he hid himself from it, even when the cost of doing so was too high for Vlad's tastes. Drac's relief hadn't lasted long.

For five years, Abraham seemed to disappear. Vlad became a man, and the birthright that should have been Abraham's had been placed on his shoulders. That was when the killings began. Making an enemy of one who knew as much as Abraham did had been their father's folly. Abraham had studied dutifully, a wide array of subjects that would allow him to lead in his time and to interact with humans intelligently about their cultures.

He'd prepared himself for the birthright Drac would never let him claim. That knowledge, combined with the lesser curse his lineage afforded him, made

Abraham a most dangerous adversary. Abraham was fast and strong, but he also knew more than any hunter alive how a vampire fought and their weaknesses. He also knew many of the individual vampires, and so their seemingly insignificant habits and minor weaknesses worked against them.

Abraham had been born and raised with the skills to lead or destroy as he saw fit. In the twenty years since Abraham's return, he'd nearly accomplished his goal, the eradication of the race he could never join.

But, hate of that depth takes a toll. For the past ten years, Vlad had watched his brother. He'd seen Abraham's disastrous attempts to conquer his hunger through a mixture of human science and the magic of their race, his melancholy and anger when he invariably gave into the urges again, and his futile attempts to be the human he was never destined to be. *Lost between two worlds, belonging to neither and coveting both.* Vlad shook his head, furious as always that Abraham had been reduced to this sorry existence. He! Why should Abraham have to endure this for so long?

For ten years, Vlad had watched, while their father turned a blind eye to the situation. Drac hid from his elder son's wrath; as Abraham destroyed the people he should have led, while he slipped into madness, while Abraham became a monster—and a widower. Vlad was forbidden to end Abraham's suffering by either means at his disposal, forbidden by a spineless coward of a leader and father who ignored their crumbling world.

Vlad sighed as Abraham stiffened. His brother felt Vlad's presence. It always happened if he tarried too long near Abraham.

It is inevitable, Vlad reminded himself. This moment had been coming for the last five and twenty years. Now, their father was dead, slain by Abraham's hand the night before. The old man's death had freed them both to the courses of their destinies. It was time.

Vlad stepped from the shadows and into the lamplight. Abraham turned, the predator in him given free rein to act. His black eyes settled on Vlad, and his crossbow came up.

Vlad forced back a shudder. This was not Abraham Tepish. This was VanHelsing, the dead mother's son. He used her name to enact his vengeance, a sign of his separation from the life he would have—should have embraced. Abraham Tepish was the man who should have led. VanHelsing was the man every vampire feared, a man powerful, relentless, vampyr born.

* * * *

Abraham hesitated, his hands shaking, cursing himself as he blinked back the tears that threatened. "Vlad," he breathed.

He'd never expected to see his brother again, never dared hope to encounter him. Drac had surely ordered Vlad away. For years, Abraham had imagined he could feel Vlad with him, but the sensation had passed nearly as quickly as it had come, an impossible wish left unfulfilled.

Abraham sobered in the realization that this was no reunion, no homecoming. Vlad was here for one reason. Their father was dead, and dealing with Abraham fell to his brother now. Vlad wasn't a pusillanimous pig like Drac had been. There would be decisive action to stop Abraham now.

"You've come to kill me," Abraham noted calmly.

Vlad's eyes narrowed, and his mouth twitched, though his expression remained unreadable. "You wish to die?"

He faltered. Abraham had wanted to die for years. Almost since the moment he had learned his birthright was forfeit, he'd wanted it, but he'd wanted his father to kill him, to take responsibility for what he'd done. Every attack on vampires had been designed to draw the old man to him, but it was all for naught. In the end, Abraham had tracked Drac down. Even as he'd trained his weapon on the bastard, he'd been denied release.

How many nights had Abraham prayed for death? And yet, faced with Vlad as his executioner—Abraham didn't want to die at his brother's hand.

There had been hundreds of encounters over the years, at least sixty dead vampires. None of them had killed Abraham. Some had tried to kill him and failed against one born and trained to be their Lord, leaving wounds that healed at ten times a human rate and left no mark, yet another bitter reminder that Abraham was not human. Some had died without raising a hand to him, perhaps fearing his father's wrath if Abraham were killed. Abraham would have welcomed death by any of their hands, but not by Vlad's.

Vlad cocked his head. "Do you wish to die, Abraham? Do you wish to join your wife and son? If you do–"

"No," Abraham snapped, fury feeding him now, wiping away the weariness that had been dragging him down moments earlier. How dare Vlad mention his wife and son!

Abraham had been a simpleton, believing human science could overcome his lineage, believing his weakened blood could spawn nothing more than human. He'd been a fool, and his entire family had paid the price of his indiscretions. He'd suspected Joseph as marked at his birth, and Abraham had refused to grant Sarah another child, though she'd wanted more desperately. That had been the beginning of the end of their relationship as husband and wife.

Sarah had withdrawn further and further, as Abraham's madness grew, as his hunting took more of his strength and time. She'd shied from him, as his rages deepened. She'd hidden her tears, as he'd pushed her away in his deepest depressions.

He closed his eyes. And then—Then came the most shameful of his failures.

Vlad nodded. "You found Joseph in the grip of the hunger you never warned him would come, trying to sate his need with his mother's blood. You loved her, Ab–"

"Stay out of my mind," Abraham growled.

"I cannot see into you, Brother. Father's insane vow or not, you are what you were born to be. You should have been given your birthright when you were a man and demanded it. I am an imposter."

Abraham met his eyes, wary. "Then, how could you know about Joseph?"

Vlad slid his gaze away, looking the boy he'd been when Abraham saw him last. "I saw it. I saw much of your life. I would have intervened if I could. I would have stopped you before–"

"Silence," Abraham ordered.

His brother quieted, but the memories filled in his meaning as if Vlad had spoken the damning words aloud.

Abraham stood, his son's blood on his hands and clothes. He felt numb, his mind still, his great logic deserting him when he needed it most.

Sarah pulled at him, the blood from the knife wound Joseph inflicted turning her blue bodice deep red. "Why?" she pleaded, hysterical. "What has happened to our son? What manner of devilry is this?"

He groaned aloud. Abraham hardly remembered now the words he'd used. They'd been guilty words, an admission of what he was—and what he'd made their only son. They were the wrong words, though he'd thought at the time that Sarah deserved the truth from him. How wrong he had been.

Abraham reached for her, trying to console Sarah, perhaps hoping that she would console him in return, that they could share their loss. She struck him hard across the temple with a bottle, an injury that would have killed many human men. Sarah spat at him, cursing her foolishness forever choosing to bind herself to him. Then she ran.

For a moment, he considered letting her go, but he loved her, and he could not release her without trying to prove that love to her. He would have promised her anything to make it right. He would have promised her children that he would train properly or even release to the realm that had shunned him. Surely, his father wouldn't have held his sons to the damned vow. He would have even knelt at Drac's feet for her.

Abraham pushed to his feet, pounding after her, knowing for certain that whatever her plan was, it didn't include him ever holding her again. Whether she meant herself harm or meant to turn him over to the very hunters he'd trained to kill vampire, there was no hope if he didn't stop her. Even as he heard her death cry, the scream of one who seeks death yet fears it as it rushes to meet her, he denied that he had lost his last reason for living.

Abraham pointed his crossbow, aiming for Vlad's heart, trembling, knowing full well that Vlad was the one vampire he could never bring himself to kill.

"Do you wish me dead then?" Vlad asked.

"No," he admitted, cursing his inability to think clearly.

His brother nodded, a smile of seeming relief flirting with his lips then disappearing again. "Good. I can be of no use to you dead."

"Use?" Abraham asked, confused by that statement.

"Why is it that you hate the hunger so?" Vlad countered.

Abraham faltered. "It is repulsive to me."

"Is it?" It wasn't a taunt. It was a simple, conversational inquiry.

"Of course. Why wouldn't it be?" Drinking blood he said was used for his experiments—Hiring the occasional whore for fresh blood—His head spun at the monster he was.

"If you had been gifted your birthright," he began.

"It would have been different," Abraham snapped.

"Would it? Because you would take the blood without needle or blade? For the rush of feeding with a body fully designed for the task?"

Again, Abraham faltered. "No. Because–" *Why?* His mind taunted him, rejecting the simple fact that he wanted what had been stolen from him.

"Or perhaps because you would be what you were meant to be." Vlad didn't ask it. His brother knew that was the truth of it. "Being cursed with the hunger and not gifted your birthright was cruel, even for Drac."

He nodded. Vlad had always known him best.

Vlad raised his arm, unfastening his cuff.

Abraham watched him, curiosity overwhelming his sense of unease. "What are you doing?" he asked.

Vlad met his eyes. "You have suffered long enough, Brother. I come to give you peace."

"To kill me." Suddenly, falling prey to Vlad didn't seem such a bad thing. It would be good to escape this madness.

He sliced open his own wrist with the fangs Abraham had always longed for. Vlad's blood welled up, rich and red.

The smell taunted Abraham's senses, calling to him. He realized he was staring, his mouth watering at the sight. It had been nearly a week since Abraham had indulged last, and the hunger was powerful.

"I come to offer your birthright," Vlad whispered, kneeling and offering his arm as if a penitent, his eyes averted.

Abraham forced a breath. Then another. "What?"

"I made no vow. Until you take your place, I am Lord of All, and he who receives the gift of the Tepish house is my choice. I come to serve the true Lord. Take what I offer or ask for the release of death. I give either freely. I pray you will choose life, Brother." Vlad glanced up at him then lowered his eyes again.

Abraham stared at him, the crossbow slipping from his hands, clattering hard on the stones, the bolt firing, ricocheting off a post. Silence fell again. His breathing was harsh and fast. His feet carried him forward, dazed, ravenous, hope warring with disbelief that the end could be so easily won.

He closed his eyes in ecstasy, lowering his face to Vlad's wrist, capturing the first taste of power and life on his tongue. Abraham suckled at the source, at the blood of a Tepish, the only blood that—willingly given—could gift him appropriately.

His head swam. His body sang, the relief of his birthright easing the aches and exhaustion. Still, the darkness claimed him.

* * * *

Vlad smiled, catching Abraham as he fell. He swept his older brother to his shoulder, carrying him as if Abraham weighed no more than a small cat.

It wouldn't take long. Abraham was a Tepish, a strong one and one destined to be Lord of All. He would wake before morning, sure in his strength, a Lord the likes of which the vampire race had not known since the days of Drac's father's father. He would wake in the home that was his now, Abraham's true place.

Vlad looked at Abraham in the lantern light, as he laid him in his bed. Abraham's face showed his age, lined and strained, but he was still regal, a born and bred leader. Perhaps, it was right that Abraham was destined to lead. A Lord should look his place. Drac had never looked older than Vlad did today, even at more than three hundred years of age.

Drac's face had seemed mired in misery and apathy for as long as Vlad could remember seeing it. Abraham had fought tirelessly. Now that he'd returned, he would fight tirelessly for their people. His face promised that. This was a man Vlad would be proud to bow to.

He looked to the window, his delicate hearing picking up the sounds of the human hunters who'd thought to meet up with VanHelsing that night in the square a block away. He smiled at their decision that their leader had fallen in battle with the foul creatures they sought, borne up by the discarded crossbow and the vampire blood at the site.

Vlad turned back to Abraham with a laugh. "Sleep, Brother. You will wake soon, a hero in two worlds. As it should be."

A Wasted Mind

September 15th, 2025

Andrew Ellison closed his eyes, repressing the urge to roar out his fury to the dark corners of the room, his heart aching even as he hardly felt the glass shards drawing the blood running down his hand. He'd broken another beaker, the seventh in the last two days. His supply had dwindled to a dozen or so, and he'd have to order more soon. A groan escaped his lips at the thought of an hour or more at the keyboard, pecking out the simple request, a stylus gripped in his uncooperative fingers, his hands shaking and sweat running down his face.

I must not lose patience again.

He looked at the shattered keyboard and monitor on Mitchell's desk guiltily. If Andrew lost his temper again, he would smash the only link he had to the outside world.

I should order another now, just in case. I should order two.

He lumbered to the sink, clumsily spinning the handle that would turn the water on. Finesse beyond him now, Andrew had come to accept that any water from tepid to scalding was better than none when you were incapable of fine motor control.

The soap slipped from his hand, becoming slick in the spray with frustrating speed. By the time he'd gotten it back into the soap dish, three faulty grips later, tears threatened. He turned the water off, finally abandoning the drip he couldn't supply the torque to stop with a whimper, a pitiful expression of his upset and unhappiness.

His head bowed, Andrew shuffled for his bedroom. In all honesty, keeping his gaze glued to the ground as he walked was a good idea. If he stumbled and fell, it might be half an hour before he managed to right himself and continue his day. If he severely injured himself...

No, he wouldn't think about that. Andrew forced his mind back to his original train of thought. As it was, it took him three times as long to rise from bed and see to his toileting every morning. Because of that, he slept now only when exhaustion left him no other choice—longing to work even as he grudgingly surrendered to sleep.

Completing his work was imperative. He'd cheated death once, and he wouldn't escape this prison that way, no matter the cost of his survival. *But how long can I continue this way?*

The answer came immediately, with more than a touch of the fury burning inside him. *As long as it takes! Until I am whole or dead.*

Andrew looked at the bed in dismay, wishing for the little things he'd taken for granted when he was young and foolish. *Does anyone realize how precious coordination and self-sufficiency are unless they have been had and lost?*

Philosophizing on useless things wouldn't get him horizontal and off to dream state. As usual, it was a fine balance between his knowledge of physics and the uncertain responses of his muscles, even when the order he gave them was a release of all tension. Once in motion, Andrew couldn't possibly react fast enough to compensate for a misjudgment. Once he'd chosen a position, it was a hope and a prayer.

That night, he landed better than most others though worse than a few. He heard the thump of wood and saw the shower of stars before the throbbing pain fully settled in. If rising again didn't mean so much time and require him to face the possibility of worse results on his next attempt, Andrew would have taken ibuprofen. Instead, he maneuvered his legs onto the bed, sighing in relief when he'd accomplished it.

The photograph of a rafting trip he'd taken with Mitchell mocked him, too high for him to pull down and Frisbee tonight as he'd done with many of the others. He closed his eyes, thinking the curse on his "friend" that he couldn't force his mouth and throat to form, slipped into sleep—and remembered.

* * * *

"It would work," Mitchell finished, breathing hard, his eyes slightly manic as they always were when he was excited about a new experiment. He motioned to the printouts in his left hand, crumpling the edges in his excitement.

Andrew smiled. "For pets, but..."

"Humans, Andy. I know it."

He pushed away his annoyance at being called Andy and forced a smile to his face. "Mitchell, you have to keep testing. You can't skimp on this."

"But–"

"A dog's thought patterns are more instinctual than a human's. You have some noted loss in ability to follow formerly trained commands. You don't know how this will affect learned knowledge in the human brain. There also seems to be some hypotonic or hypertonic effects occurring sporadically in the test subjects. Those need to be fully explored before you consider moving to humans. What if..." Andrew paused, reluctant to crush his friend's hopes of becoming a Nobel winner in the next decade.

"If?" Mitchell asked, tension clear in his jaw.

"To gain permission for human testing, we'd have to prove a minimum of neural damage in lower animals. Not just dogs and cats, but primate subjects."

"There *is* a minimum of–"

"We don't know how much there is yet. What if you get permission to bring a child back, and you bring it back with severe brain damage?"

"An adult–"

"Frankenstein's monster, buddy. Can you imagine some poor woman who expects her husband restored as he was. This isn't something you can flirt with."

Mitchell seemed to contemplate that for several long moments. He turned to the windows overlooking the bay and set the printouts on the work table.

"Let me run tests," Andrew offered.

"What kind?"

"Body chemistry to go along with your brain functionality testing. On every animal you've brought back and on all future subjects, before and after the procedure."

Mitchell sighed. "It's the right way, I suppose."

Andrew nodded, relieved that he wouldn't have to beat this one through Mitchell's skull. "Yes. It is the right way."

"Let's do it."

* * * *

September 16th, 2025

Andrew opened his eyes, wincing at the throbbing in his head and the dull ache in his fingers. He struggled out of bed, cursing his uncoordinated state.

It wasn't a matter of strength; Andrew had proven that for a fact. The problem lay in his ability to apply the right amount of pressure steadily and reliably, to control his body as he always had—before.

All the little things he'd learned as an infant and toddler were torture for him now. His hand-eye coordination was almost non-existent, the processing of his motor and sensory at a marked discontinuity compared to "normal." Simply passing an object hand to hand was a chore. Forcing his muscles to work in the smooth, rippling flow of the athlete he'd been was a physical impossibility. His confident stride had been reduced to an awkward shuffle. His muscle tone was shaky at best. Even his lovely baritone was no more.

Some days, Andrew cursed Mitchell for what he'd done.

Then common sense intruded, and he refused to retreat. Unless he wanted to spend the rest of his life as Mitchell Silver's monster or resign himself to death, Andrew had to keep working on a treatment. No matter the state of his body, he had his glorious mind, the mind that had launched him into college at thirteen. In the end, he hoped that his mind would prove the salvation of his failing body.

He couldn't remember dying.

The sound that escaped his throat was halfway between a snort and a sob, the most appropriate noise he'd made for anything in a long time.

On some level, he was glad he couldn't remember dying. Was that something any sane person wanted to remember?

When he'd woken from death, Andrew had been confused, terrified, living in anguish and frustration. He'd believed Mitchell's story then. Mitchell was his friend; he'd done what he had to do to save Andrew's life. It had been an allergic reaction, acute asphyxia. Defibrillation and CPR hadn't worked, even after the shots of epinephrine and adrenaline. It was Mytaxin or nothing, Mytaxin or death.

Mitchell's heartfelt horror at Andrew's condition had seemed sincere—at first. He'd worked diligently, following the steps Andrew had painstakingly laid out in hopes of treating the aftereffects of Mytaxin, the effects he had suspected but never understood fully until he was afflicted personally with them.

But the treatments he'd formulated hadn't stabilized the nerve functions as they should have. Torturously, Andrew had directed Mitchell to change after change that did nothing to reverse his unresponsive body.

It was then that Andrew saw through the lies—or rather that Mitchell confessed everything in a raving fit. Andrew would have been happy to believe the lies to the end if it meant that Mitchell really meant to help him reclaim his life.

The asphyxia, if it *was* asphyxia, was caused by some drug Mitchell had used. It was unlikely that his "friend" had tried anything but Mytaxin to save him, more likely that Mitchell had done nothing but sip his wine and watch Andrew die with a self-satisfied smile on his face, timing the moment when he'd administer the injection with precision.

Mitchell's rant had laid it all out for him. Darvis Pharmaceuticals had been too close to a breakthrough of their own. He'd been mad in decision, driven to win as he'd always been driven to win. Andrew's insistence on the slow approach would lose them the race in the end—unless Mitchell forced a human trial, unless he gave Andrew a pressing reason to correct the problems that might occur. But Mitchell hadn't counted on the treatment eluding Andrew as long as it had; he saw his dreams of market conquest failing, and Andrew took the blame, the scapegoat for his partner's madness.

Andrew grumbled at his reflection, thinking the words his tongue and lips would no longer form. His face was gaunt and pale, overrun by an unruly beard and moustache he couldn't properly shave and a mass of knotted hair he was incapable of grooming or cutting. His blue eyes were over-bright in darkened sockets over a nose he'd broken twice in his months alone and a mouth that always hung slightly agape when not clenched shut.

His numb fingers fumbled at the soap, then the toothpaste. The toothbrush, fisted in his hand as if he were a preschooler, gouged his sensitive gums and soft palate more than once each in his attempt to keep more of his teeth from rotting away. They ached from improper cleaning and were cracked from his frustrated grinding and his poorly-coordinated attempts at chewing food. In a rare show of pity for himself, he decided to forego a shower and change of clothing. After all, who was there to impress?

The trip to the kitchen exhausted him. He'd been awake for all of forty minutes, and it felt as if he'd run a marathon. His eyes misted up at that, and he forced himself not to waste more energy by crying useless tears.

How much longer could he stand living this way? Every day brought him closer to the point of no return, the point when the damage to his body from his existence in this state would outweigh any recovery he could find for the condition. Already, it would take months of physical therapy to regain a fraction of the prowess he'd once possessed. Some of the scars he'd amassed would never fade, and his teeth... Pulling them and replacing them with ceramic would be kindest.

Marathons were a part of his past, and he had to face it. Every day in this decrepit shell amounted to more of his former abilities that would never return. He just prayed that he would someday find a treatment that might allow him to care for himself and walk with a cane. The realization that there might never be more was sobering, but he would be alive and able to work with assistance. After his enforced hermitage, an assistant sounded like dearest heaven to him.

When will I become the monster and nothing more than the monster?

Andrew pushed away the thought that he held to strained strands of humanity as it was. He looked the monster, felt the lumbering beast, and he had certainly acted the monster more times than he could count in the months he'd been cursed. He wouldn't consider the things he'd done. If he argued the right and wrong of it again, he might give up and kill himself before he was discovered and the state did it for him.

I am not a monster! I was provoked, threatened, pushed beyond reason. Of course, he'd been.

For now, it was time to eat and work. His dreams would bring memories of the beast set loose in him. That was more than enough punishment without heaping on conscious consideration.

* * * *

May 2nd, 2026

Andrew groaned. How long had it been? How many months? Did he dare count them? Did he want to?

He'd lost pieces of three teeth in the last week and had started chewing aspirin directly into the pits to bring relief from the constant pain for a day or two at a time. The acetyl and spiraeic acid did more than kill pain; it burned away the nerves inside the teeth to keep the pain from returning in the usual two or three hours swallowing it accomplished.

How ironic that was. He'd been fighting all this time to heal his nervous system, and now he was killing what few nerves worked. His harsh laugh came out a series of guttural seal barks.

Eating was a torture now, even when his teeth were blessedly silent. He'd lost so much weight that his shorts and sweats hung low on his nearly skeletal hips.

Weary of injuring himself over and over, he'd managed to drag his mattress to the center of the bedroom floor, an effort that cost him an entire day of work. There, he collapsed every night. Even if he rolled off the edge, the springs would break his fall and minimize his discomfort when he landed on the cold wood. It took twice as long to get up from the floor than it would from the bed, but that hardly mattered.

Even using paper plates and cups had ceased to make his life tolerable. His muscles had degraded so that even getting trash to the furnace was beyond him. The entire house stunk of rotting food, sweat, and chemicals.

His hair was matted and filthy, home to a forest of insects he couldn't wash away, available chemicals to do so or not. Or perhaps, the crawling sensation was simply a phantom, a trick of the mind he was certain was slipping. Either was possible, and there was no way to know for certain.

Even the ability to raise his arms to rub shampoo through the chestnut tangle was beyond him, and he was lucky to manage a shower twice a week these days. Insects were a very real possibility. Then again...

Men were never intended to live in such isolation. When he'd had his mind intact in a reluctant body, he'd had hope. What did he have now? His mind was wasting away to madness, and he could no longer deny it to himself.

It was time. It was long past that precious moment of no return, though until the day before, he'd never dared admit it to himself. Even if he found the magic mixture today, he was beyond help.

I was beyond help the last time I saw Mitchell.

Had he ever dared admit that?

Never.

But it was true. Perhaps his mind had been slipping since the moment he'd been revived.

No. Surely, madness would have been a happier state than this living hell.

Still, I have been damned to madness since Mitchell...

Had Andrew ever doubted that there was truly no return? Even if he'd made himself whole again, Mitchell would have ruined his reprieve and stolen his life from him eventually.

Andrew grasped the small vial in trembling fingers, trying to convince himself that it was the effects of the Mytaxin making him quake. He was lying to himself, and he knew it. He was a coward, afraid of what he'd face when death took him a second time.

I can't live like this.

Suicide is a sin.

So are many of the other things I've done. Either way, there is no heaven for me, though there may be peace of another sort. The only hell he could conceive would be a continuation of his "second life." Surely there was no punishment worse than that.

He brought the vial to his lips and drank down the contents, losing only a little from the corner of his mouth. It didn't matter. Andrew had put three times what he'd needed into the vial, anticipating some catastrophe that hadn't materialized—for once.

It won't take long, he soothed himself. *A few hours, at the most. A relatively painless end to so much suffering.*

But he wouldn't die in this sty. Andrew intended to die breathing fresh air, the sun on his emaciated face.

He shambled out the door, leaving it open. The animals could help themselves to all that was left. The printout of his letter to the authorities was hung safely on the smashed computer monitor. Anything else, he had no use for—including the corpse he'd leave behind.

At the young birch tree, he lowered himself painfully to the ground, the soft bark peeling away as he slid, slipped, and fell to his knees, then his arse. Andrew panted, thanking God that he wouldn't have to live this way anymore. He said one final prayer for forgiveness, pleading a seemingly hopeless case for his black soul.

He deserved heaven. He'd done his best to rectify this situation. Before he'd filled the vial, Andrew had smashed the vials of Mytaxin in the sample sink, pouring chemicals and water in at random until no analysis could be made of the damned mix. He'd burned all the written work and DVDs save the ones of his condition. Leaving those was a reminder of why no one should try to follow Mitchell's work. He'd even scrubbed all the data from his former partner's computer with a garbage overwrite to ensure no one could retrieve it later.

I did everything right. There will never be another monster like me, if I can help it. I deserve peace! I could have done worse things—much worse.

A tear wound down his cheek, and he patted the ground beneath him. Yes, he'd considered much worse things. How many times had he considered filling a syringe of Mytaxin, digging up Mitchell and making him live in pain for the minutes or hours until his decaying body gave out again? Then filling another syringe and repeating the endeavor until his sense of outrage had been appeased? Some days, it would have taken several injections, watching his partner die more painfully each time, to appease him, but he'd never stooped that low.

He'd killed his friend quickly, in self-defense, crushing his spine and ribs.

Too much pressure. I never meant to kill him. I simply had no control over how hard I clenched my muscles.

Liar! Of course, he'd meant it. Mitchell had turned him into an experiment, a beautiful mind trapped in a nearly useless body. He'd stolen everything from Andrew: his work, his recreation, even his freedom. And then he'd sought to kill his creation, his disappointment, the monster he'd once called friend.

I was provoked! Endangered... That much was true. There was no denying it.

And there was no use arguing it—even in his mind. Andrew closed his eyes, surrendering to the warmth seeping into his muscles. He would die, but he would die more a man than a monster. He couldn't ask for more than that.

* * * *

May 5th, 2026

"Such a pity," Daniel Darvis sighed, pitching the last of the DVDs the police had brought him back into the box with Andrew Ellison's letter.

If only Ellison had come to him for help, he'd be a healthy, productive member of society now, much as all the successful patients treated with Recombix IX were. According to the evidence, Darvis's breakthrough in dealing with neurotransmitter decay came relatively early in his affliction. Ellison could have been their banner case. Now he was a piece of meat chewed on by various predators and scavengers, big and small.

"What a waste of a brilliant mind."

One-Hour Burial

Why put yourself through the rigors of a public viewing for the deceased? Why expend any more time than necessary with an odious task? With our simple, computerized form, you can choose from three interment options in the comfort of your own home, enter insurance information, and rest assured that everything is in order. At Winters' Funeral Home, you stay at home, and we take care of the rest.

Errol Winters owned the only drive-through funeral business in Maine. It had been intended as a stunt, but the zombie mist had changed that. These days, you had to bag, tag, and bury them in cement within six hours, or else your ass might just become zombie chow.

That changed the entire business of death. There was no time for an extensive examination by the M.E. these days. No one did autopsies. Most corpses got nothing more than a cursory "Looks like a gunshot wound to the chest, Joe." before chucking the sucker at Errol and running for the hills. More than a few murders had probably gone completely unnoticed, because no one wanted to be within a hundred yards of a corpse when the six-hour incubation period was up.

No one visited grave sites of former loved ones. No one held wakes, because there was no question that the deceased would be moving in short order.

There was no time for embalming, which meant—ironically, in this time of the zombie mist—Errol went home smelling much better than he had months ago. His wife Ellen liked that well enough.

She liked their bank account even better. What had started out as a gimmick to drum up business had turned into their golden egg.

Ellen hadn't liked his choice of an assistant much, but she got over that. Danielle Stevens, Danni for short, was a looker, but Errol hadn't hired her for her pretty face.

The fact that she could hold up her end of the containment box, should it fall off the rollers and that become necessary, was a bonus plan. But the clincher had been the always-ready firearm on her hip. Danni had won a sum total of half a dozen sharpshooter trophies in middle school and high school, between handgun and rifle. In an emergency, she was going to take a head-shot; there was no doubt of that. And only a head-shot would do.

Not to mention, there hadn't exactly been a glut of takers, when Errol went looking for a replacement for Matt. The money aside, no one sane wanted to do this job. Errol and Danni were decidedly less than sane, these days.

The drive-through facility afforded them safety in dealing with the zombie incubees...or whatever it was George down at the morgue called them these days. The medical examiner, now the proud owner of a ton of free time, was writing a book on the zombie mist. That was fine; Errol was fairly sure George wouldn't make half as much money on his book in a year as Errol was making every month in one-hour burials.

The system was perfect. Joe, the local Sheriff, would pull a truck into the drive-through and stuff the pertinent paperwork into the bank deposit door. Then he'd muscle the deceased into the seven-foot-long, three and a half-foot wide, three-foot-high metal collection box, padlocking it in five places, just in case.

On the off chance someone's clock was off on the time of death or a body hadn't been discovered in the first hours after death, that box could be pushed down the rollers and into the crematorium for instant disposal. Errol did that when he had to, but truth be told, roasted zombie smelled worse than embalming fluid, so it was the cement bed, when they had the time for it.

As long as the box stayed still as death used to be, Errol and Danni would mix up the cement and start it pouring into the lined holes prepared for the quick turnaround burials were these days.

It hadn't taken long to figure out their safety zone. There had to be at least two feet of quick-dry cement on all sides of the metal coffin. Most everyone opted for three, for good measure. As long as the coffin was covered before the howling, growling and thrashing started, there was no way the beastie would get out before it set up, good and solid.

A month or so in the cement, and they died...or at least they went into some sort of hibernation. No one had been brave or stupid enough to dig one up and find out for certain which it was. Errol didn't have any burning urge to be the first.

Some quick prep, a metal box, some padlocks, and a whole lot of cement earned Errol a cool twenty-five grand per planting, less Danni's cut of three grand. If he actually had to roast the sucker, it was thirty-five grand, five of it to Danni, because of the "added risk of dealing with the undead lashing out." In actuality, there was no added risk, and he could reuse the metal collection box, but Errol and Danni both sure hated that smell.

The current "client" had seemed no different than any other. Joe dropped him as fast as possible and bagged ass, like usual. Errol and Danni set up the cement and rolled the coffin down, dropping it into the mess. Then they started covering it with the rest of the cement, joking about a job well done.

The first few squeakings and squawkings made them distinctly nervous, but the truth soon settled in. Half a foot from the top and muting almost all of the sound from inside the coffin, the cement was covering what was surely a live specimen. Live! Not dead. Not undead, but rather live and breathing.

Danni turned off the flow, listening to the indistinct shouts. She swallowed hard, looking to Errol in misery. "What do we do? Dig him up?"

Errol considered that. They'd known this was bound to happen someday. With the rush through the formalities, some poor schmuck was sure to be pronounced "dead," when that wasn't the case.

Heck, it would be the perfect murder. Give someone an overdose of some sedative and call in Joe... As jumpy as they all were, someone could miss the faint signs of life. It was probably a miracle this one had woken up while they were standing next to the grave.

"Errol? Do we dig him up?" Danni was squirming in place, looking more than a little rattled at the screams from under the cement.

He hooked a thumb under his cap and tipped it up, shaking his head. "By the time we get him out of there, he'll be dead of suffocation anyway, and we'll just have to bury him again." *And, we'll be covered in cement and dog tired, for the effort.* "He was a big one. You saw Joe shove him in there. Must weigh more than three hundred. There's not much air for him."

Danni nodded, taking several deep breaths. "Should we let Joe know it might be a murder?"

That answer came quicker. "You want someone to exhume the zombie to prove it?"

His assistant's face went pasty. "Hell no, boss. He can stay in there."

"My thought precisely."

Errol turned on the cement again, watching it fill then overfill the grave. Yes, the zombie mist had changed everything about the business of death.

Stay With Me

Why did I answer the phone? It was all in fun, but I should have checked caller ID and skipped this one.

"So, are you going to sell?" Rebecca asked again.

Shawna pulled her sunglasses off and smoothed the unruly cap of curls on her head, playing one dark curl between her fingers as she met Jonas's eyes. Every few months, it came down to this moment. At least, Rebecca wasn't here at the house this time. Jonas was always more upset when Rebecca came to the house to ask.

"We've discussed this," he grumbled dangerously. "Nine times."

Rebecca sighed a long, tortured sigh.

"I know," Shawna mouthed. "Rebecca, why do you continue to ask? How many times have I said no?" *Why do I bother to ask?*

"Ten," she growled before Shawna had finished the question. Rebecca didn't need to *hear* the question to answer that.

"It will be eleven," Jonas intoned.

"They've doubled their bid," Rebecca pleaded. "It really is too much house for you."

Jonas made as if to snatch the phone from Shawna's hand, but she dodged him smoothly. She put up a hand to still him, and Jonas crossed his arms over his chest, his jaw tight in fury.

"No," he reminded her sternly. Jonas would never stand for them selling this house.

Shawna nodded. "I'm sorry—"

"Think about it," Rebecca requested, cutting her off.

Jonas snorted in disgust.

"I will," Shawna promised. She disconnected before Jonas could become more upset.

He nodded slowly. "We're not selling." It wasn't an option for Jonas. It never was.

Shawna sighed. "Does it matter? We'd be together anywhere," she soothed him.

"No. We'll be together here," he insisted.

She sighed. "Rebecca is right, you know. It's too much house for us. You know we can never fill it with children the way we planned."

Jonas moved suddenly. He took her shoulders in his hands, a grip that felt almost real, his hands muted through her silk blouse. His deep blue eyes were pain filled, brimming with unshed tears at that reminder.

"If I could change that, I would. You know I would."

Shawna ran her fingertips over his sandy beard, remembering the feeling of it on her breasts, teasing her as Jonas thrust inside her. They'd had so many hopes then—before the accident. If only she hadn't asked him to delay having children— No, she wouldn't think about that now.

"I know," Shawna whispered.

"Close your eyes."

She groaned, complying with his request. Jonas's lips feathered over hers, tasting her. Shawna never truly understood why it was more real this way, but it was.

Jonas was fierce, hungrier than he had been since the first few times after the accident. Shawna wound

71

her arms around his shoulders. His beard rasped over the sensitive skin of her chin. The taste of him was so delightfully potent—sweet iced tea with lemon.

He backed away, folding her hands in his and leading her toward the house silently. Shawna went with him, her feet finding the path through the rooms unerringly as they always did. They'd done this many times in the years since the accident. God willing, they'd do it many more.

She kept her eyes shut tight, reveling in the feeling of Jonas's solid hand in her own. Shawna knew better than to open her eyes, knew Jonas wouldn't open his. It hadn't taken them long to learn the rules of their existence. The psychic had helped with that.

When one was a spirit and one was flesh, hard choices had to be made. This was one of them. They could draw on the strength of their love to make the faint recollection of touch a reality but only if their eyes remained closed to the truth. If they gazed at one another, the moment was lost, not to be recaptured quickly or easily.

People always said that the blind made up for their loss with their other senses until what was lost was barely missed. People lied, but it was the price they paid for touching each other, and so they lived with it. It was maddening.

Shawna smiled as the hardwood floors disappeared and she felt the rug under her bare feet. Jonas's hands pulled at her buttons, his breathing harsh. She ran her hand over the length of him straining against his trousers, wringing a groan from him.

Shawna sobered, imagining the look of urgency on his face. She would give anything to look in his eyes as he loved her again.

Her blouse fell away, and Jonas's hand stroked over her stomach up to her breasts. He massaged her nipples to rigid points, making her gasp in the rise of pleasure between them.

"Remember?" he breathed. "Remember when we bought this house?"

"Yes." She did remember, stumbling into the bedroom, locked in a passionate kiss, falling together onto the rug—the only thing they'd moved in at that point. It had been an hour before they moved anything else.

Jonas's mouth closed on her breast. His tongue was insistent, stroking her as only Jonas could. Shawna unbuttoned her skirt, pushing it down over her hips and letting it fall. Jonas pushed her panties after it.

When a lover died, it was likely for the survivor to move on, their minds accepting the loss, even as they denied it consciously. The survivor rarely wanted the burden of the deceased soul. He or she rarely acknowledged the hovering presence, the responsibility for filling the void in a life ended too soon, the pain of choosing between seeing and touching, the agony of lost hopes and dreams. The spirit lived in longing for the sensations lost, physical and emotional touch, whether the survivor granted the spirit ease or not. Sometimes, the survivor's need was as strong as the spirit's, as it was with herself and Jonas. It was both a blessing and a curse.

She cupped his face up to hers, meeting Jonas's mouth, ravenous for this connection, for these moments stolen from the deep recesses of time.

Too long. It has been too long.

He led her to the bed, easing Shawna down onto the knit sheets. Jonas rose off of her, the rustling announcing his clothes leaving his body.

Shawna shivered at the depth of his need. Jonas was desperate. The thought of a life without her, no matter how short or long, filled him with terror. Even if Shawna's need didn't match his own, she could never ignore Jonas's pain, even with the fathomless pit of death between them.

Jonas sank to the bed beside her, his fingertips making trails along her inner thigh. "We decided this when your family sent the psychic here," he whispered.

Shawna nodded, arching to his hand, shivering as he breached her body. "They were worried," she gasped.

"Yes. They were. Even the psychic had a hard time convincing them that we were happy this way. They wanted you to move on to something better." His fingers played at her, twisting and massaging inside her.

She grasped his shoulder, writhing beneath him. "No," she pleaded. "Jonas, I need—"

"Remember why we stay here, Shawna. Remember for me." His lips trailed down her stomach.

Shawna spread for him, begging for what he offered. Jonas was always like this when Rebecca tried to convince them to sell, and sex was never better between them—except that they couldn't use their eyes.

Jonas's talented mouth had always been one of his most endearing traits. Shawna trembled as his tongue flicked over her clit. That was the first taste of Jonas she'd ever had, and the moment was burned in her memory.

Their first date had been a roller coaster ride. The tension between them had risen, painfully slow. They'd had dinner and drinks, a few fleeting touches. When Jonas asked to take her home that night, Shawna hadn't been prepared for how quickly he would own her—body and soul. Her body had fallen quickly, as easily as this. Jonas's hands and mouth enthralled her, shattered her. Then he'd possessed her, and they were both lost...or more appropriately, found.

His tongue flicked again, teasing her, taunting her, reminding her why they would never leave here.

"Tell me, Shawna. Tell me why we're staying here." He traced her seam slowly, knowing from years of practice what would keep her on the edges of ecstasy.

Shawna swallowed, trying to wet her dry mouth. "The psychic," she stammered.

"Tell me." Jonas tasted her, moaning into her body.

"The spirit is strongest in familiar surroundings."

"And?" he whispered into her, making designs over her with the tip of his sinful tongue.

"The stronger the memories, the stronger the connection."

She bit her lower lip as Jonas buried his tongue deep inside her. He stroked slowly, trying to drive her over now that she'd laid out why they wouldn't leave this house. She couldn't lose Jonas again. Shawna couldn't face the pain of those first few days without him again. She couldn't live with the thought of existing without him in her life.

"If we leave," she continued slowly, "it may not be this good between us. We may not be able to touch each other anymore, despite our love."

Shawna arched her back, as Jonas became more insistent. Was it desperation at that thought that drove him, or was he rewarding her for her recitation of the facts? Was it a plea not to set them both adrift by forcing the issue and leaving this house? Shawna was afraid to question that too closely, afraid that she wanted to set Jonas free. She didn't. She couldn't.

"Our," she gasped. "Our memories are strongest here, in this room. We can have it all. Just because we—" She fisted her hands in his hair.

Jonas's beard tickled her thighs. He brushed his moustache over her clit while he took her deeper. She had to finish the discussion. Shawna had to assure Jonas that she didn't want to leave him or their home.

"Just because we can be together away from here for short periods doesn't mean it will last without—" She cried out as he forced her over, unable to hold back another moment.

Jonas settled over her, his cock parting her. "Without the memories—the energies we charged this place with," he finished for her.

She nodded, her lip trembling. "I can't lose you again, Jonas."

"Stay with me. Promise me."

"I will."

Jonas thrust deep, groaning as she wrapped her legs around him. His length filled her, stretched her.

Jonas had always fit her as if he had been carved to match her precisely.

Shawna met his body, losing herself in their shared pleasure, imagining Jonas's face. She longed for the times when they spent whole afternoons in this bed: touching, talking, gazing at each other as if they beheld a crystal ball that held the answers to eternity.

They cried out together, as Jonas climaxed deep inside her. He pressed her into the bed, his mouth urgent against hers, trying to hold to this moment as he always did.

"Never leave me," Jonas whispered. "Don't make me live that again."

Images exploded in Shawna's mind, coming unbidden and unwanted at the worst possible moments, as always.

Jonas was driving. Shawna laughed at a joke he made, batting his arm playfully.

"Oh, shit," Jonas shouted, yanking the wheel to the right.

Shawna looked up, frozen in disbelief. The truck was coming at them, riding the center of the narrow road.

"Down," he ordered, pushing her head down to shield her with his shoulder and chest.

The first impact was to the driver's side front quarter panel. Shawna screamed as the car spun, bouncing off the guardrail and skidding on the wet pavement. The motion ripped her from Jonas's side, and she hit her head on the window beside her. She looked up blearily at the sound of a horn blaring.

The next impact was to Shawna's side, a Mack truck that crushed the car around it like a Coke can. The glass shattered—all of it flying like deadly raindrops through the passenger compartment. Shawna felt ripped from the world, as pain and darkness took her.

Her eyes flew open. She had to see Jonas instead of the darkness.

Shawna shook her head, screaming her loss as the sensations deserted her. Jonas was over her—in her. She knew it. She felt the phantom whispers of his touch but nothing more.

He opened his eyes, misery etched on his beautiful face. This was the pain she caused him. If Shawna believed that Jonas would be happier, she'd find a way to release him—to live with the pain, but he wouldn't be. Neither would she.

She touched his face, the scar that reached from the center of his left cheekbone to the corner of his jaw below his ear. Shawna ran her eyes over the spray of scars on his shoulder.

"Shawna," Jonas cried out. "Shawna, please answer me."

She forced her eyes open, her body wracked in pain. Blood ran down his face and neck, seeped through his dress shirt. He seemed covered in blood, his and hers alike. His eyes were full of tears.

Shawna tried to touch him, but her body was unresponsive. She shivered, chilled.

Jonas took her hand gently, his tears spilling over. "Don't leave me," he pleaded.

* * *

Jonas stilled, holding Shawna, though he knew she couldn't feel him anymore. Her translucent body shook in sobs beneath his. "Shhh," he soothed her. "It's over."

She nodded, her dark eyes misted in the illusion of tears, the memory of crying. He wept with her—for her, tears Shawna hadn't been able to weep in two years.

It had been a senseless accident, a drunk driver who crossed the centerline. Had that been the end of it, he'd still have his wife, alive and in his arms. The eighteen-wheeler couldn't have stopped.

Shawna had literally been crushed, broken. She hadn't lived long enough for the firemen to cut them free. For the first week, Jonas had wished he'd gone with her—until Shawna learned to reveal herself to him.

"Why?" she whispered.

Jonas didn't have to ask what she meant. Why did he accept this life when he could go on? He couldn't bear the thought of that, of living without her as much as the thought of making her suffer for wanting him until he joined her. "We've been through this."

"'Til death do us part." She stroked the cool wisps of her fingertips over the scars on his chest. "You deserve children and dinners out and—"

"Shhh. We've argued this. I deserve you. I want you, as I have always wanted you. Tell me you still want me, too."

"But—"

"Death didn't part us. That should tell you something. Stay with me."

Shawna nodded. "I want to."

"Then I'll call Rebecca and tell her no."

A mischievous smile curved her lips. "Let me."

Jonas laughed. "Why do you insist on doing that to me?" he asked.

Rebecca couldn't see or hear Shawna. Only the psychic and Jonas could hear her. Only they could touch her. Shawna's family could only see the misty image of her—when they tried to see her. Usually, the sight of her was too much for them.

Only the psychic understood why Jonas stayed. To everyone else, he was a slightly crazed hermit, running away from life since he lost his wife, maybe even blaming himself for the loss. Little did they know that this was the only life Jonas wanted.

"You are so funny when you're covering for me," she admitted.

Jonas laughed. "Promise me forever."

"I did at our wedding. What's changed?"

He shook his head. "Nothing. Nothing at all." *More importantly, nothing ever will.*

Once Upon a Blue Moon

"Once in a blue moon," Val mumbled, pulling her knees closer to her chest.

"No jokes tonight," Carl answered.

"How many hours until daylight?"

"Too many." Her older brother shook his head, making his tight, blond curls bounce. "You would have to date a werewolf. What were you...high or stupid?"

She shifted uncomfortably. "He's not so much a wolf. More a big dog."

"Good. We'll cage him between the camels and the elephants."

"Works for me. How many hours until dawn?" she asked again. She'd look at her own watch, but weredog drool seemed detrimental to wristwatches.

Carl ignored her, concentrating on the tome in his hands instead. "The book says... Man, these suckers are hairy. You never noticed? I thought you didn't like hairy men?"

"He's not," she protested. "You know I wouldn't have given him the time of day."

"Maybe he waxes," he quipped in reply. "So where did you meet this guy?"

"Remember that trip to the peat bogs of the British Isles? Well, he was with another tour...I think."

He arched a brow at her, a classic big brother move. "You think?"

"Well, we both sort of left the tour there. I grabbed my gear and he grabbed his. And...and..." Her face burned, and she was suddenly thankful for the darkness.

"Yeah, thanks for not supplying the TMI. I don't need to hear about nipple clamps and Vaseline."

"Oh, come on! You know I'm not into nipple clamps. I don't do pain. I don't even wax, because I'd rather deal with nicks than ripping out hair at the root."

A smile curved Carl's mouth. "I notice you didn't protest being into Vaseline," he taunted.

"You promised to help me," Val reminded him, reining in the last of her calm.

"I am helping."

"Picking apart my sexual tastes is not helping."

"Oh, then you are into Vaseline?" he persisted.

"I'm not into Vaseline. Now, Astroglide... Oh, what am I saying? Just get me out of this!"

"How could you pick up a guy in a peat bog? Beyond the smell factor, don't you know what kind of weirdos hang out in those places?"

"Hey! I like peat bogs."

"Well, that certainly proved my point," he offered sarcastically.

"Carl, will you stop being an older brother for two minutes and help me figure out how to solve this?" Keeping her voice calm when she wanted to smack him and drive a stake through Adam's heart was difficult.

Or is that one vampires? Val had never been able to keep those supposedly mythical beasts straight. She'd been too busy keeping the real ones straight...like ghosts and fairies. Then again, if werewolves were real, who knew what else was?

"Just tell me one thing. Did he at least do it for you?"

"Fireworks and all," she admitted. She'd never been more satiated.

"A dog?"

"He wasn't a dog when we were..."

"Doing the horizontal bop?" he suggested.

Val grumbled a couple of comments about men in general and brothers in particular. "Discussing this is getting us nowhere. What does the book say about --"

"Weren't there any signs that this guy was abnormal? I mean more abnormal than you are."

"Well, he could eat spaghetti loaded with garlic, if that's what you mean."

"That's a vampire, Val. Could he go near Wolfsbane?"

"I wasn't exactly looking out for any."

"What were you looking at, then?"

"His ass, if you must know. He has a great ass."

Before Carl could reply to that, another voice interrupted their discussion, a voice that made her heart skip a beat.

"Well, I'm glad you still think so."

"Adam?" she asked. "I thought you were..."

"Only while the moon is in the sky, and it's behind the mountains now. Unless you plan to drive me there, you're quite safe. Actually, you were always safe with me."

"Yeah, just getting drooled on," she accused him.

"Oh, I'm sure you can forgive that. I honestly lost track of time and forgot tonight was a blue moon. You make me forget that anything exists but you. If it makes you feel better, we can mark them on the calendar and you can lock me in a room every time one comes up. It's only a few hours, and..." He stepped into view, his smile highlighted in Carl's flashlight beam. "I rather like restraints, as you well know. I can take them as well as give them."

"Vaaaal," Carl complained. "TMI."

She laughed heartily. "I didn't say it." Gods, how could she doubt Adam for a minute? "I make you forget everything else, huh?"

As if he gleaned his cue in there somewhere, Adam dropped to one knee and raised a ring box into the stream of light. "I humbly offer myself to you, Val. You know I could never hurt you. Wolves mate for life, you know. That's why I couldn't hurt you when I changed. Had you been anyone but my mate, I would have ripped you to shreds."

"Then you knew I was already?" she asked in surprise. They'd only been dating for two months. Even she wasn't sure he was right for her, though she'd been arguing it with herself earlier that evening.

He grimaced. "Well, no. I thought you might be, but this confirmed it for me."

Carl huffed out a breath. "So, you put my sister in that sort of danger."

"He forgot," Val defended him.

"I forgot," Adam protested at the same time. "See? That's what I need a mate for. Val is order personified."

"Val forgets where she left her car keys ten times a day," Carl countered.

Adam shot him a shit-eating grin. "Yeah, but she knows her cycle better than I do, and I usually have the advantage in that department."

"TMI! TMI! TMI! Wait...what advantage?" her brother asked suspiciously.

"My sense of smell. How do you think I found her tonight? I can smell Val a mile away...three when she's fertile."

"Oh, come on, Val. You cannot possibly be considering this. You want to have puppies?"

Adam shot him a look of confusion. "They'd only be cubs at the blue moon, and Val can look on that as Mommy's night out. I know my mother did. She didn't think it was all that catastrophic."

"Val --"

She made a noise of consideration. "Mommy's night out. That's not so bad. Most of my friends would kill or steal for one of those once in a while."

"I'll throw in every full moon, though it doesn't have the same effect," Adam offered in temptation.

"Make that a girls' night out on the same day until we have kids, and you have a deal."

"It's sort of a tradition that our kids are conceived back home," he continued. "I thought you might like to know that."

"The peat bog?" Carl guessed.

"Don't ask where you were conceived," Val warned him. "Mom told me. Besides, that means I get to see Europe again...at least a couple of times."

"Val, please tell me you're kidding," he pleaded.

She stood, dusting off her jeans. "Oh, come on. He's no worse than Uncle Matthew and his Doberman that wants to have me for lunch."

Adam growled at that. "No one threatens my mate."

"Better tell Uncle Matthew to leave Grizzly at home," she mused. "Anyway, he's strong, sweet, protective, intelligent, definitely faithful..."

"Don't forget rich," Adam teased.

"Which reminds me... You owe me a new watch."

"Would you like gold or platinum?"

She tucked her shirt in. "With you around? A Baby G."

Adam stood, towering over her. "That's a yes?"

"No!" Carl answered for her.

"Yes," she replied patiently.

"Val!"

"Oh, go ask Mom how you were born. While you're at it, ask her why she planted flower circles in the garden."

She smiled sweetly and walked away, letting Carl digest that one.

The Punishment of Phoebus Apollo

"What would you have me do, Father?" Phoebus Apollo shifted, turning his face away from the pitiful creature on the grass below, contempt shining in his eyes. He scowled. "I do not invite this fascination."

Zeus sighed. "Show her pity. You know what she craves. Would it harm you so much to go to her?"

"Why should I see it again?" he grumbled. "She craves the brilliance without reason and without care of the consequences she courts. It is always the same. They want to know the true brilliance, to bask in its glory, heedless that its intensity will leave them charred, a husk of their former selves, lifeless at my feet. Why should I endure it again?"

"To give them peace," Zeus explained patiently.

"What of my peace?" There was no exhaustion in his tone, only determination.

"You will not concede?"

"Never," Apollo vowed.

He sighed. "Go on then. Begin your journey." Zeus turned his gaze back to the girl on the grass below. She was there as she was every night before the sun rose, waiting patiently for Apollo to begin his journey.

Apollo turned on his heel and glided away, the vision of the perfect god and yet still lacking. He had forgotten mercy in his arrogance. It was a harsh lesson to relearn.

Zeus stretched his hand over the mortal realm, his heart aching at what he had to do. He could not change the essence of a soul, only its form.

Apollo's cry of rage and pain shook the heavens.

Zeus nodded. His son had seen the results of his folly.

The sun moved more rapidly than usual that day, Apollo driving his steeds hard to rejoin Zeus at Olympus. Zeus waited for his arrival, knowing the argument to come, knowing that his son would likely hate him for his part in this matter, for the choice he'd made to bring Apollo to heel.

In Apollo came, burning now in fury instead of his typical glory, his beautiful face a terrible mask. "Turn her back," he demanded.

Zeus folded his hands carefully, as if in deep consideration. "I cannot. You know I cannot."

"How could you do this?" he thundered.

"It was the most merciful thing I could do for her. Clytie's essence is unchanged. Still, she blooms in your light. Her face follows your progress across the sky." He met his son's eyes. "As the sunflower, she always will. The one bloom will become many, Apollo. Soon, you will see tens of her shining face. Hundreds. Thousands on every journey."

Apollo weaved on his feet at that, paling. "Why?" he pleaded. "Why have you done this to me?"

Zeus stared him down. "You should have shown her mercy. I gave you the chance to do so. Always remember the cost of my mercy, Apollo."

Trick Or Treat

Sean slid from the bed, careful not to wake his younger brother as he pulled on his trousers and padded down the hallway to the front door. The house was quiet. It was a night not even the most hearty of men braved, not even the stoutest ventured outside, for you never knew what vengeful spirit you might meet on Samhien.

His Gran explained that most spirits were playful, mischievous, merely glad to have a night where their feet touched the moist soil and their tongues tasted the sweet offerings left on doorsteps. Others were mourning life lost too soon or even enraged at those who'd wronged them in life – or any mortal who walked in the sun and had breath in his lungs. Those were the spirits even the stout men feared on the night when the two planes touched.

He paused at the door. Of course, Sean feared as any man would. They'd all been told from the cradle what terrors a night like this held. Perhaps he feared more, since he was only ten and seven. Perhaps not, since he was considering doing what few men ever did.

Can you live with yourself if you do not do this?

A fine tremor started at his shoulders and worked through his body. "No," he whispered. Fear or no fear, he had to do this.

Sean patted his pocket, assuring himself that the package was still there. It would never do to go without a gift. Relieved, he let himself out into the night silently and raced across the clearing to the edge of the trees.

He'd barely set out the napkin laden with sweets when he felt it, a presence beside him that made the hair on his arms and neck stand on end. "Lisabet," he breathed.

Sean didn't question that it was she. Surely, she'd dreamed of this night as he had. Or...did spirits dream? That was neither here nor there. Surely, they wanted, else there would be no spirits longing for life lost. And, that was what drove him here, the mad need to know that Lisabet was not in pain where she was now.

"I brought you your favorite chocolates," he told her, still not meeting her eyes.

Coward! Sean winced at that. He was a coward. He was terrified that Lisabet would show use of her illness, pockmarked and drawn – or worse, worm ridden and decayed from her months in the grave. *If you meant not to look at her, why did you not leave your offering at the door as the others did?*

"Do you hate me, Sean?" Her voice cracked at that, and a sound halfway between a sob and a breeze moved between them. "Do you fear me?"

He forced his gaze up from the frosted grass, unable to cause her more pain. She'd already known more than her share from life, stolen away in the blush of youth. Lisabet had only this one night of the year to taste life again. No matter what her state, he would give her ease.

His breathing hitched. She was beautiful, pale as when he saw her last, before her illness had made itself known in other ways and she'd been quarantined.

Her hair was pulled up and back in a deep green
ribbon that matched her eyes, curls cascading down
over her shoulders.

A sob stuck in his throat, and tears stung his eyes.
"I could never hate you," he admitted. "I had to see you
again."

Lisabet nodded, her eyes filled with longing, a
longing he'd hoped he wouldn't see. "Do you miss me
very much?" she whispered.

"I do. Every day." It was no secret that he'd hoped
to marry her one day, but she'd not lived to a
respectable age to ask. A few more months... But,
they'd not been granted that long. "And you?"

"I am surrounded by souls though not the one my
soul pines for. I have only this night and then I must
leave again."

"And I must watch you leave," he sighed.

"There is no one else then?" she asked in surprise.

Sean smiled wryly. "How could there be?" How
could he look at another now? How could he ever?

She swallowed hard. "Would you..."

"Anything," he vowed. Anything that would ease
her time, he would gladly do.

"In life... You never kissed me, Sean."

His heart pounded in anticipation and unease
mixed. Was such a thing possible? Would she be cold
as ice? Would she taste of the soil she was buried in?
Did he care, if it would make her happy for a single
moment, the only moment she had for such a thing?
He had to chance it. He had to know.

Sean nodded, barely breathing as she leaned
toward him.

Her skin was warm and soft, her lips like satin against his. She tasted of late berries and smelled of pies and spice. He ran his hand through her curls, threading his fingers around the dangling ends of the ribbon as their kiss grew more passionate. A mad wish to have her like this forever assaulted him. If only there was some way...

No one in Dunn's Corners questioned how it happened. From the moment his mother's screaming woke the rest of the house and the nearby farms, it had been clear to all.

The official cause of death on the Medical Examiner's report was exposure. A silly teenaged boy who hoped to see ghosts on All Hallows Eve had ventured out in near-freezing temperatures with no coat or shoes and died from the cold, the hijinks of youth gone tragically wrong.

The Medical Examiner had overlooked the length of green ribbon in Sean's hand and the half-eaten chocolates at his side. If he noted them at all, he'd probably rightly assumed that the boy had gone to find Lisabet on the night he died, though the city-educated man would dismiss the idea that he had found what he sought.

A year later, a tray of the same chocolates Sean had bought with his birthday silver graced the front stoop of the home that had once been his. Through darkened windows, two women watched the young couple eat the sweets, laughing and kissing, forever beautifully in love.

"He could not live without her," his mother sighed, wiping away her tears.

His Gran shook her head, clearing the sudden tightness in her throat and patting her daughter's shoulder with a gnarled hand. "And, she could not die without him."

Anima Ex Machina

"Twenty-seven," Adrienne muttered, jogging to keep up with her older sister, Jen. There was little time left to get the details Dr. Sander demanded; in just a few minutes, Jen would be engrossed in solving the Net tears, and there would be no talking to her then. "I don't understand how Alex is doing this." As their only remaining tenth-level programmer and Alex's former team leader, Jen was the only one who might hold the key.

They passed the twenty-eighth floor. "By exiling him, I gave him access. He *is* tenth-level. He's rewriting the code from the inside out."

She shuddered involuntarily. No one had ever considered the possibility that it could be done. "Can you stop him?"

Jen glanced at the uplink screen on her braceband, punching up another alert, speeding past the twenty-ninth floor as she entered a macro response code.

"He's tearing Net Central apart, Jen! The power grid, communications, transportation, even safety systems have gone haywire. Can you stop him?"

"Yes. I can."

Adrienne breathed a sigh of relief, turning into the thirtieth floor and Net Central a few steps behind Jen.

Guards scattered at their approach, and seventh-level programmers shouted out status figures for the failing systems that all of mankind depended on. What would they do if Alex took it all out? How would they survive a week without Net Central's support?

Jen stripped off her jacket and headed into the V-R room, nodding to one dire prediction after another, already planning her counterattack.

Adrienne followed along, taking the jacket from her sister's hand then a V-packet from a frightened-looking tech. "You're going inside? Isn't that dangerous? If Alex is tearing holes--"

"Power up," Jen commanded. "He's recoding from inside. The fastest way-- The *only* way to stop Alex in time is to go in."

She nodded, setting the jacket aside and tearing the packet open with her teeth.

Jen already had her shirt and shoes off and was settling in the chair. She spread a thick layer of the electrolyte gel on her face and neck, moving to her chest as Adrienne unpacked the interface cables that would pick up the subcutaneous nerve impulses directing the program, in effect making her sister's entire body a tool.

"It was the hardest thing I've ever had to do," Jen stated, hand entering the console commands for the procedure she intended.

Adrienne faltered then forced herself to focus on the task. She didn't have to ask what Jen meant, but it wasn't something they typically discussed. Whether or not she'd even discussed it with the debrief counselor was an uncertain thing. 'Hard' didn't begin to cover the trauma Jen had faced. The betrayal she must have felt... The anger must have been incredible. She'd hated Alex for making her do it.

"I loved him, you know," she continued.

"I know, but there was no alternative. Alex would have killed us all. Stranding him inside was the right choice."

"Was it?"

Adrienne stared at her, stunned to silence by the misery in Jen's blue eyes.

"What if we were wrong, Adrienne? What if -- I misjudged him?"

She placed the last two cables, her hands shaking. Had Jen ever doubted herself before? Perhaps, but she'd never said it. "He's trying to finish the job, Jen."

"Can you imagine what it must be like for him? Alex is a lone, sentient being trapped in the Web. He's..."

"What?"

Jen removed her braceband and handed it off, slipping her hands in the reader beds. "Frustrated, lonely, maybe half-mad."

"You can't go in there," Adrienne whispered. *Screw your service record. Screw the whole world.*

Jen pushed the prep button inside the reader, and the overhead lights extinguished, leaving only the blue glow of the command center.

"Synch in sixty," Net Voice informed them.

"What will you do?" Adrienne asked.

The alert flashed on Jen's braceband as it had countless times in the last six hours. Adrienne punched it up; it might be information Jen would need inside.

"Synch in forty-five."

Jen,

Please, answer me. Please, tell me you're coming. I need you. I love you.
Alex

"Dear God," she gasped. How long had he been contacting her?

"I'm coming, Alex," her sister whispered.

"Synch in thirty."

Adrienne launched toward command, scanning the program Jen had loaded in horror. She tried to override, but Jen had used her higher access protocols to lock Adrienne out.

"Synch in fifteen. Shield down."

The protective plas barrier came down, the shield that would keep anyone from tampering with the V-R chair while a programmer was virtual. Adrienne hit the wall, kicked it, shouted for someone to bring her a crack bar.

"Don't do this, Jen! Can you hear me? Don't..."

"Going virtual," Net Voice intoned, an impassionate announcement of her sister's death.

Adrienne sank to her knees, hitting the plas again, a half-hearted blow punctuated by her sobs.

Cheers went up from the main room. She'd done it. Jen had saved the day, as usual. But this time, the heroine of the people wasn't coming home.

"Full integration of psyche complete," Net Voice announced.

Adrienne closed her eyes, nodding, hating her sister for doing this. There was a fine line between love and hate. Maybe Jen knew that better than Adrienne had counted on.

Phantom Dreams

Dedicated to...
*Sissy and Nana...*who wait for me behind the veil.

"Sleep well, mon petit chou," Papa whispered, closing the door to her bedroom slowly, so as not to disturb her when the lock caught.

Ines feigned sleep as she did every night. In truth, her heart pounded in such anticipation that sleep was impossible. It wouldn't take long. Jacque always came for her moments after her father left for the night, seeking his own rooms in the opposite wing.

There was nothing sinful in Jacque stealing into her room this way. The man *was* her husband, after all, and had been for nearly two years. She furrowed her brow. More than two years now, though how much more she could not say for certain.

"Till death do us part," she whispered.

She sighed at that. Death had parted them, yet not. It was that one fact that made Ines hide Jacque's nightly visits from her father.

She was mad--or going mad. There was no question of that. From her assignations with her dead husband to the phantom cries from the far reaches of the house, her sanity was suspect.

Then there were the memory lapses. She had no memory of the daily routine of her life, no grasp of the mundane tasks of eating, dressing or bathing, though she was rarely hungry, always dressed appropriately in one of her many gowns, and invariably clean and well-presented. She supposed the head injury she sustained might explain that, but most likely not.

Her entire existence seemed to revolve around her evening reading, the occasional discussions with Papa, and Jacque's visits to her. Or...perhaps it was the only portion of her day that held meaning for her, the only moments she wanted to remember. If so, she was even more melancholy than she thought.

"My love."

The bed shifted slightly, as Jacque stretched out beside her. Ines had ceased to question how it could be so days earlier...or perhaps it was weeks or months earlier. Along with the memory lapses, her grasp of the passage of time seem strained.

At any rate, if she was going mad, what was the point in questioning her perceptions of the seeming physical presence of Jacque's body in this place? *None,* and so she dismissed her uncertainties.

His lips traced hers, making her hunger for him. "Open your eyes, dear one," he breathed. "I know you are awake."

She tried unsuccessfully to hide the smile curving her lips, so happy that he was with her for a few short moments that she could not help but join in his teasing. "Hmmm... Rather full of yourself," she suggested.

"You do not wish my company? Very well. I will take my leave."

Her eyes flew open as the bed shifted, and she grasped at his shoulders, shaking her head. Pure terror coursed through her. If Jacque believed she didn't want him, he might not return, and her loss would be complete.

His smile disappeared. Jacque leaned over her, dragging the light quilt off of her as his lips covered hers.

She closed her eyes, imagining another time like this one, a time when Jacque had no words as he took her, his tongue patiently parting her lips, the joy between them a living thing they could not wait to see...

No! She would not think of that night--or any night before Jacque was taken from her.

He released her mouth, pulling up at her nightdress and tossing it toward the door. *A nightdress I wouldn't have worn in our own bed.* Ines pushed the unwanted observation away. She had only these moments with him, until the meager strength she'd regained failed her and she slept again; it would be a sin to waste even a moment on such thoughts.

He was tender...at first, a sweet reminder of the earliest days of their marriage. But she was the nervous virgin no longer, and soon they were entwined on the bed, bringing each other bliss in a frenzy of touching and tasting.

He knew exactly how to touch her, and he used his knowledge well. He explored the lines of her body slowly, sensitizing every fingerwidth until the moans muted into the heel of her hand gave way to heartfelt cries she stopped trying to quiet.

She blushed at the idea of her father hearing their passion, though he would be in the opposite wing, and the house was full of rugs and heavy wood that would mute even the loudest of her screams over that distance.

Jacque's kiss grew impatient, and he locked their bodies together...stilling then seeming to regain his composure. He rocked inside her slowly, and Ines grasped at his hips, pleading silently for him to send her into bliss. He chuckled, denying her.

"Jacque," she gasped. How could he do this when he knew her stamina would not stand for it? If he continued thus, neither of them would know release before she lost her tenuous hold on consciousness. It had happened before, and she cursed herself soundly when it did.

"No, my little one. You know what I want from you."

Her mind rebelled, though her body wanted completion enough even to do what he asked. He asked the same thing every night, and so far, she had failed him.

It was fear, she knew. If she relived that awful moment, what would happen?

He promised he'd stay with her always if she did, but what if he lied? She was torn on that point. Part of her argued that Jacque would not lie to her. Another reasoned that he would if this limbo with her were painful enough for him.

Was she hurting him? Perhaps holding him here when his soul ached to pass on to his Heavenly reward?

Ines opened her mouth to ask him bluntly then stayed her tongue in shame and misery. If Jacque was in pain... If she knew it, she'd feel compelled to release him. She was a selfish and unworthy wife to do something that might harm him, and yet the thought of never seeing him again was too much to bear.

Still, Jacque moved within her, his expression hopeful. "We were in the carriage," he began in a solemn voice. "Night was falling."

The snow dotted path flashed in her memory. "Please," she begged. "Please, do not make me see this."

He ignored her plea, pushing on as he always did. "You wanted to stay, but I convinced you to go."

Jacque smiled, a playful smile that announced he would have his way. "The snow will keep us here far too long. Were you not the one who said you would not give birth without Sarah and your own bed?"

"Jacque, I cannot..."

"You must, Ines. You must remember. For us."

She ran a hand over their child.

A lightning flash of pain made her vision blur. Ines whimpered. She could always feel her injuries at times like this, the cracks in her skull most of all.

A girl! The baby was a girl!

She panted, her mind muddled. How would she know that? As far as she knew, no one had ever discussed the baby with her. Had they? Had she forgotten her own child?

The pain assaulted her again, and she arched her back up, pressing down hard on his elbows.

"Drink, Ines!"

The voice was there and yet not. She couldn't seem to recognize it.

Bright light blinded her, and her entire body ached. Her breathing was strangled. Motion made her dizzy, and she choked on a cry of agony. Pain exploded in her back, radiating through her injured ribs, though her breathing became less labored. She coughed harshly, suddenly flat on the bed and splayed out, her chest heaving with each shallow breath.

She raised her hand minutely, her strength fled.

Where was Jacque? Had he left her? Why had she choked that way? Did he stop it? What was going on?

Her eyes slid shut, and blackness stole all thought and sensation.

* * * *

Ines snapped awake, the novel she'd been reading lay open in her lap. She ran a shaking hand over her face.

The nightmares were almost worse than the damage to her mind. Ines didn't have to ask what they were. She'd pieced together enough information from them to discern that her injuries had been severe. Thankfully, she had little memory of her convalescence, though her dreams seemed intent to reveal it to her in detail. What little she remembered was enough to make her wonder at God's tender mercy.

She winced at the completely irreverent thought that there was nothing tender in the pain she'd felt and nothing merciful in her survival when all she loved but Papa had died. It was sinful to question the Lord. Ines vowed to confess it as soon as it could be arranged.

Or had she confessed it a thousand times only to think it again? How many times had Papa brought a priest to her here, since she could not travel to one, to hear her beg forgiveness for this single traitorous thought? Never? Ten times? Every day of her life since Jacque, and she remembered none of it? The thought chilled her. How could she know what was real and what was not?

Was her time with Jacque before the nightmare part of the dream? Was he truly here, and she lost consciousness, lived a day she could not remember only to fall asleep reading and dream horrid dreams of her recovery that wiped away everything before until there was no pause from one to the next for her? Or was she simply mad, and none of this was real?

She tested her faculties. She felt the warmth of the fire, the cool smooth wood of the chair. She smelled the smoke. No. This was no fantasy. Fantasies were not this real. She groaned, wishing yet again that she understood what had happened to her, that she could rationalize her inability to separate the two.

A knock came at the door, tentative, almost questioning.

"Come in, Papa," she called out, feigning interest in her book, so he would not worry.

He entered, smiling though his eyes didn't show it. "Would you take company with me?" he asked in his thick accent.

"Of course," she managed brightly. When had she ever refused him? She pushed away the thought that she might have refused him many times.

He started across the room, and panic assaulted her. Why were her only memories of this room? Did she ever leave it? Were her meals brought to her here in the belief that she was too weak to come to the table? She scrambled to her feet, and her father looked at her in concern.

"You are well, mon petit chou?"

"Yes," she lied. "I should like to walk with my Papa. Perhaps, we could speak in the library." Ines waited patiently for his answer.

His smile returned--and lit his eyes. "I should like," he agreed.

The corridors were empty, almost eerily quiet, making her wonder how late in the night it was. Were the servants abed already? True, Papa only kept a few servants, and only three in the house. The cook never ventured past her domain. One maid worked only downstairs, but the other... She fought for the woman's name.

Blanche?

She winced at the twinge of pain even that exertion caused her.

Blanche would work on this floor. Did she ever see the servants? Perhaps in those lost hours? Did she even know for certain that Blanche was still in Papa's employ? She didn't, and she didn't dare ask him and reveal how little of the daily workings of the house she could remember.

Ines could find no words to fill the void. In truth, there were many things she wanted to ask, but the answers would be painful, and whatever horrors she faced and forgot during her convalescence had made her wary of pain.

In the library, she took a seat. Her father sat across from her, seemingly concerned.

"What is it, Papa?" she asked, clasping her hands in her skirts until they ached.

"I am overjoyed that you chose to leave your rooms, though I worry that you may tire."

She winced. She'd been right, after all. "I will more often," she vowed. "It may help strengthen me."

"That is good." He said no more, waiting as he always had since the accident, letting her speak first.

The questions circled in her mind until she felt certain they would drive her to madness, if she weren't already mad. "Papa," she blurted out, blushing deeply.

"Yes?" he asked, his expression one of surprise.

"My baby-- My baby *was* a girl, was she not?"

He stared at her in stunned fascination. Papa moved abruptly, dropping to his knees on the carpet between them. Ines started to protest that he would hurt himself with such antics, but she stopped in shock as he scooped up her hands and kissed them, tears in his eyes.

"You remember the bebe," he whispered.

"No," she admitted. Her heart ached as if it would burst in her chest at the admission, but she forced herself on. "But, I remember... Oh, Papa! I believe I remember she was a girl." Tears wet her cheeks. "Why can I not..." She sobbed, a hopeless wish for everything to make sense to her welling inside.

He gathered her to his chest. "Shhh. It will take time, but remembering is good."

"Why? Why would I want such memories, Papa?" She wanted memories, but not those memories, not the ones Jacque insisted she latch onto.

"Start with the bebe, Ines. See your daughter."

She closed her eyes, trying to picture her child. Did it have her sunlight curls or perhaps Jacque's rich brown locks?

"Hemorrhaging..."

There was blood everywhere on the bed. The sheets were soaked with it.

"Why now?" a woman wailed.

For a moment, Ines locked eyes with Blanche.

"My Lord! She sees me."

"She cannot see you," a man snapped. "Help me."

Ines found herself in Papa's lap, weary and confused. What had she seen? Was that horror her daughter's birth?

"You did not see her." Her father didn't question it.

"No. I did not." She sighed, closing her eyes. If only she could sleep, she might dream of her child instead of the pain of her recovery.

* * * *

The room was dark around her, silent. She was thirsty, more thirsty than she could ever remember being. When she reached for the pitcher of water on the bedside table, the pain in her chest and abdomen exploded like white-hot embers. Ines screamed, her hand fisting around the cool porcelain handle. It tipped off the table and slipped through her boneless fingers, shattering on the floor.

Voices rose and fell as footsteps rumbled ever closer. Ines screamed one last time as a strange face hovered over her, passing into darkness.

* * * *

Ines covered her face with her hands, groaning into them. Did she dare try to understand that memory? Perhaps it was a memory of her labor. Perhaps the man was the local doctor. It had been years since either she or Papa had seen a doctor at his home.

Her nightgown announced that her father had prepared her for bed--or had a maid do so. Or, had she accomplished it herself and had no memory of it?

Frustration welled in her. She was through with her predictable existence. Like her walk to the library, everything would be different, if she could help it. Ines stripped off the nightgown and stuffed it under her pillows, pulling the quilts up to her neck and feigning sleep as her father approached her room.

The door swung open with only the slightest protest. "Sleep well, mon petit chou," he whispered, closing the door and disappearing down the hall.

Jacque was there in moments. Ines didn't give him time to explore and learn her secret. She pushed the covers away, a sensuous slide down her body, uncovering herself to him.

He stared, seemingly frozen in disbelief. Ines smiled sweetly and pushed him to his back.

* * * *

Jacque caught her head between his hands, meeting her offered kiss hungrily, groaning at her passion. It had been so long since he'd felt her fire, it strained his control.

Better, it was new. He knew she'd ventured out of her rooms with Pierre, her Papa. He knew she remembered little Yvette. Now she met him without that loathsome gown and pursued him sexually. Perhaps, she was ready to abandon this half-life she'd sentenced herself to.

She broke away and met his eyes. His heart ached at her beauty. Ines was whole again, unspoiled by the tragedy--in body. She could be whole in mind, if she chose to be, if she embraced her memories and let go of the past to start anew with him.

He opened his mouth to question her. Though he wished it wasn't necessary, she was finally showing signs of progress. If he could end her pain, even by causing her a bit more, it had to be done.

Ines covered his mouth with one pale hand, her eyes sad. "One day," she whispered. "Please."

Jacque nodded, kissing her fingers. It couldn't hurt to allow her a moment of relative peace.

Her smile returned, and she eased along his body, crawling backward like a cat retreating along a fencetop, graceful, sensual, teasing him unmercifully.

It was a game they'd played many times, and Jacque knew it well. It was a test of how long he could stand it, but it had been too long for him. He wrapped his hands in her hair, his mind muddled, half-ordering her come to him, half-pleading for it. Jacque cried out harshly as she complied, glad that he hadn't ruined this moment with questions that would drive Ines back into her shell--or into that hateful place she had to abandon.

She was diligent and thorough, tending his passion with practiced ease. At last, he gave in to the call, spending in her. Ines slid from him, making her way shakily to his side. Her skin was nearly without color, a sure sign that she'd overextended her meager reserves again.

Jacque sighed as her eyes slid shut, kissing her lips tenderly though he knew she couldn't feel it. Ines had slipped into her personal limbo again, the foul place that allowed her to hide from all, existing not in her past, present or future. Though his existence was timeless now, every moment his beloved spent locked in this state was a torture for him.

* * * *

Ines opened her eyes, staring at the ice-patterned windows in confusion. It was winter again? That hardly seemed possible. How long had her convalescence been? Or, perhaps it was *still* winter. No. Her injuries had been too severe to have healed so quickly.

She sighed then winced at the pain ripping through her chest. Ines started to raise her hand to investigate, but it was held fast to the bed.

Her mind cleared enough to make horrific connections. She *felt* pain. It wasn't a memory or a dream of pain. She tasted a foul film in her mouth. She smelled sweat and sickness. She wasn't dreaming. Why had she never noticed this before?

Worse, her hands were tied down. Ines tested that to be certain, panic settling in her mind when leather cuffs cut into her wrists. She relaxed her arms into the mattress, her heart pounding as much from that mild exertion as from fear.

Think! She had to think, despite the sick pounding in her head. What explanation could there be for this?

Perhaps her life as she had come to know and accept it, her life with Papa and the ghost of Jacque, was a dream, hallucinations brought on by medication, pain, and her head injury. Her head throbbed as if in agreement. Perhaps, she was truly alone, and Jacque would not warm her bed now that she knew it.

No! Ines would not accept that it was so. She could not. Her mind reasoned that it was not true, a torturous path full of flashes of pain not unlike those she experienced when Jacque questioned her. She forced her mind to function when her waning strength pushed her toward sleep.

She felt in her "other life" as well, tasted the tea Papa sometimes brought her--and Jacque, smelled his male musk, felt his body moving in hers. It wasn't possible that both were real, but how could she know which was?

I have gone mad, she decided miserably. She'd known that it was a possibility, feared that it was true. That must be why she was tied down. This was reality, and these people knew she was insane.

Ines shuddered in the realization that she would gladly retreat into the other world with Jacque and Papa, even if it marked her as mad. She groaned at the jolt of pain the movement set off. It seemed her entire body ached.

"Ines?" Blanche's voice came from far away.

Her face was blurred, as if viewed through a haze. Ines fought to answer her, but the words would not come. Her breathing was labored, painful.

"I knew you could see me," she whispered, her hand touching Ines's. "I know you can't speak, but if you could..."

Ines tried to squeeze her hand, but her fingers barely moved.

Blanche sobbed. "I knew."

Exhaustion dragged her down, and the room faded away. For a moment, there was silence and peace.

A baby cried.

Ines opened her eyes to the dim light of the dying fire in her room, free of pain in the other place and time. She ran a hand over the nightgown she wore, the same nightgown she'd stuffed under the pillows before Jacque arrived. She no longer bothered to make the distinction between whether or not he was a dream, certain that it was a mystery she would never understand.

How much time had passed? Or had it passed? If this was a dream, time would not exist.

She sat up in bed, striking the headboard then rubbing her hand, wincing. She felt. The sweet scent of flowers from the table teased her nose. She smelled.

The infant's cry came again.

I hear it!

Ines eased from the bed and padded toward the door. Mad or not, she could ignore that no longer.

* * * *

Jacque patted Yvette's back and left the room, confident that she would rest for some time. Their daughter was too young to understand her existence in this place. She'd latched onto the souls she instinctively recognized as her own, knowing only with whom she belonged, and so it terrified her to come up from her limbo and find herself alone.

For now, the limbo had its advantages. In time, when Ines stopped retreating into the nothingness, perhaps Yvette would as well. Until then, he and Pierre would comfort her as well as they could, though they paled in comparison to a mother's comfort.

Pierre was waiting for him in the library, staring into the fire sadly. "You did not try," he grumbled.

Jacque rubbed the back of his neck. He'd learned not to question how Pierre knew these things. "I could not deny her a moment of peace," he explained. "She begged for it."

"You wanted to love her without interruption! You are no longer of the flesh, Jacque. You do not suffer from a mortal man's complaints."

He nodded, half hating the man for demanding this of him and half-aching that he was right to chastise Jacque for allowing her to continue to suffer.

"You say that you do not wish to cause her pain, but Ines *is* in pain," Pierre continued. "Every opportunity that you let slip away prolongs it. You know she goes there. You know she feels needless pain. If it were only the nothingness of limbo..."

"I notice you do not waste your precious moments with Ines, forcing her to painful memories," Jacque shouted.

"When she allows, I do. She hides herself from me much more than from you."

"And so, it falls to me to do this to her," he complained bitterly. Jacque uttered several sacrilegious oaths. He wryly noted that it was a little late to worry about punishment for it.

Pierre merely raised an eyebrow. "Yes. It does. It is our duty to protect Ines, even from herself. To end her pain... It must be done quickly."

Jacque sighed. "How long will she hide this time?" he wondered aloud, though he knew there was no quantitative answer that could be given or understood.

"She is already stirring."

He startled. "Why did you not tell me?"

Pierre waved away his concern. "Perhaps we go to her too often. We give her little time to think for herself."

"You said only a moment ago that we should waste no opportunity to draw her out," he argued.

The door opened and Jacque stood, turning to it in shock. For a moment that seemed even more timeless than this place, they stared at each other.

Then Pierre's voice broke the silence. "Come in, Ines. Your husband was on his way to you."

She staggered, falling to her knees, shaking her head in seeming disbelief. "I *have* gone mad," she breathed.

Jacque strode to her, fury driving him on. He couldn't let her think such a thing, and the damned missing pieces of her life were all that were needed to prove to her that she was not. He sank to one knee, drawing her into the shelter of his body.

She ran a hand over his linen shirt, tracing the line of buttons as if his clothed state confused her. Perhaps it was the idea of a "ghost" needing such things that confused her. It certainly wasn't his choice of garments, since he'd chosen to wear what he typically did relaxing at home: dark woolen breeches, polished black boots and a linen shirt.

"You are not mad," he informed her.

"Neither is she sane," Pierre offered in a grim, disapproving voice.

"Pierre," he growled. Jacque would not allow him to play games with her mind. Not now. Not when they had an opportunity to win her trust.

"She must do this, Jacque. Ines is here, living as she has not lived for some time."

"I am mad," she repeated.

"You are not," Jacque insisted. She wasn't. She simply came into this existence in an unnatural way.

"Jacque," Pierre began in a harsh tone.

"Quiet, old man," he snapped.

Ines sobbed in his arms, pressing a hand to her head, announcing that her two worlds were close to touching again. "The other place is my true life." She was tortured by the thought, her voice breaking as if she'd hoped it was not.

"They are both real."

Her eyes slid halfway shut, and she went boneless in his arms, her skin fading to gray. "It is not possible," she slurred, retreating again.

No! Jacque couldn't allow it again. There had to be a way to keep her here. He shook her once, hard, attempting to shock her into their world fully again. "No. You must face us. You cannot continue to hide away." He winced at Pierre's nod of approval. This wasn't for Pierre. This was for Ines, and if the old man had any sense at all, he'd stay out of this.

* * * *

"Jacque?" He'd never used force on her, and it stunned her that he would.

He sighed. "You know the other...place," he began gently.

She nodded.

"What do you know of it?"

"Only that I hurt. I am a prisoner there, in my body, in my mind, and in the room where I am kept. I can do nothing. I cannot even speak. I--believe I am still in convalescence." Her heart sank as he nodded to statement after statement, only showing surprise that she considered herself a literal prisoner in that place.

Ines sobbed. "I am--"

Jacque's mouth covered hers, too real and heartfelt to ignore. The kiss moved from softly seeking to passionate in moments. He drew away, laying a kiss on her brow.

"You cannot survive there and yet you try, because you fear to give yourself up fully to this reality."

She looked to her father, shaking her head in confusion, praying that he would say something that made more sense. He said nothing, only watching her with interest.

"This place is what you dream it to be," Jacque continued. "You have not relinquished the image of yourself alone here with Pierre in this place, and so that is what you see."

Her head ached, and her vision blurred.

Jacque's fingers bit into her arms, and she cried out. He rubbed the spots gently, his eyes full of pain. "No, Ines. I cannot allow you to deny this so simply."

She sucked in her breath, clarity bringing unwelcome connections. "Then Papa is not real? I am dreaming him?" Had she been interacting not with a mad creation of her husband but a mad creation of her father?

Neither of them answered her.

"Jacque--"

"You must accept and move on," he repeated.

"I do not know how to die." How did one order a broken body not to breathe? How did one relinquish the Earth? It was not something that was taught, and Ines had no idea how to accomplish it. She'd thought it was a natural step. The body died, and the spirit moved on. If she was fighting, as he claimed she was, to live, she had no sense of doing it and so could not cease.

"You must give up the thing that holds you there," he replied simply.

"How? What holds me there?" Perhaps Blanche? The kind maid's responses were wonderful, the only bright spot in the moments of anguish. Ines wanted to grant her that. Was Blanche holding her there? If so, how did she relinquish the urge?

"Just remember."

She nodded, though remembering still terrified her.

"It was nearly dark, and you wanted to stay, but I convinced you to go," Jacque began as he had many times before.

"It will be dark before we reach home," Ines reminded him. *"Cold. Perhaps icy."*

"Ines?"

"Yes. I remember. You wrapped quilts around me despite the cloak and woolen gowns I wore that night." The image of it filled her mind.

Papa kissed her cheek and waved them away, striding back toward the house as the carriage lurched down the frozen mud track. The wind was bitter, and she buried her face in the quilts.

117

Her head came up at an odd creaking sound. Jacque pulled back on the reins, but the effort came too late. The sickening snap of metal startled the horse, and it bolted, ripping the reins from his hands, free to run now that it was disconnected from the carriage, its harness broken, most likely by the cold weather.

The sudden motion of his body sent the carriage to one side. Jacque pulled at Ines, no doubt hoping to cushion her fall to the road rather than chance their slide over the hillside.

Again, a man's fastest wasn't nearly fast enough. Ines screamed as the carriage tipped then started to roll, forcing him against her so that Ines was squeezed between his larger body and the high back. Jacque flew from the pitching vehicle, roaring out in protest as his grip on her faltered.

Ines shook her head, rejecting the image.

Jacque forced her chin up, meeting her eyes. He didn't have to repeat himself. She felt her cheeks heat.

His face softened. "What did you see?"

"You-- When the carriage flipped..."

He nodded. "I know. Tell me what you saw."

"You tried to hold to me, but you were ripped away."

Jacque disappeared, swallowed up by the darkness and hidden by the spiraling carriage, momentarily airborne.

The carriage crashed down again, and the rail she hadn't realized she'd been holding snapped free as the wood splintered. There was no time to wonder when she'd grasped it or if she'd slowed their escape by it. Before a proper question could form, a sudden movement sent her tumbling into the snow. The cold shocked her awake, though exhaustion from her ordeal made her crave sleep.

Ines started to struggle against the quilts, watching the carriage come for her, an uncaring giant with her in its path. She screamed, closing her eyes as it crushed down onto her midsection and ribs then her head. Then it was gone. Blackness closed over her, and the pain was forgotten.

She had no concept of how long the nothingness lasted, only that the cold and pain forced her eyes open again. Her head felt as if it were split in pieces. Her ribs protested every breath. The skin on her knee felt rubbed away, and various other pains shot through her periodically.

Ines could force herself to do little. Though the wind was bitterly cold, she could not drag the quilts over herself to seek warmth. Though she felt the need to scream, she could scarcely draw breath.

Her mind locked on one burning question. Where was Jacque? Pains shot through her head and down her neck as she turned her face to look for him. He was above her on the hillside, and she rested for a moment as she surveyed him.

She rejected what she saw, even as her mind reasoned that the odd angle of his neck and the wide, vacant eyes could only mean that he was gone. Ines longed to touch him, but she lacked the ability to move even the few arms' lengths that separated them.

Warmth between her cheek and the snow drew her mind momentarily from her grief. Blood! There was blood on the snow around her. Ines closed her eyes, wishing for death. If it meant an end to her pain and following Jacque, she would welcome it.

"Here!" The voice came from above her, closely followed by the sounds of crunching snow and murmured voices.

Ines opened her eyes, sobbing at the sight of her Papa and one of his grooms, a young man whose name she couldn't recall.

"Heavenly Father, she's alive," the groom exclaimed.

Papa didn't respond to that. He fell to his knees beside her and started wrapping her in the quilts. She managed a strangled cry as he lifted her into his arms. Ice pulled at her hair, breaking free of the ground stubbornly and slapping against her face at the ends of frozen locks of hair.

"Shhh. Still, mon petit chou."

"Is it wise--"

"Wise? She will freeze here," he thundered at the young servant. Papa turned and started trudging up the hillside.

"Monsieur, I can help--"

"Non. Go for the doctor...quickly, Jean." He paused, a pained expression on his face. *"And call..."* He paused again, as he often did when he searched frantically for a word in English.

"Of course," Jean assured him. His footsteps faded into the night. The sound of hoof beats seemed very far away.

Papa struggled up the hill with Ines in his arms, his breathing labored. With no way to get her onto his horse without Jean's help, he started the long walk back up the path.

"I will care for you," he whispered again and again. *"I will not lose you."*

Ines forced herself back to Jacque, sick in understanding. She stayed for Papa, without knowing why she did. What would losing her do to him? It was no wonder that she fought so hard. "It will kill him," she whispered. "Oh, Papa!"

Jacque grimaced. "Do you remember anything of our daughter's birth?" he asked.

How could he ask such a thing of her now? "Jacque! Do you not see--"

"Yvette first," he ordered.

"Why? Why must I see my family stolen from me?" she demanded. "I do not want to see more."

"And so, you suffer needlessly. Pierre took you to your old rooms..." His eyes pleaded with her to continue.

"And called a maid to assist him until the doctor arrived...Blanche."

The horror on Blanche's face told Ines more than she wanted to know. It was hopeless. The other woman didn't need to speak the words.

She wasted no time, cutting away clothing and wrapping Ines's head in towels to staunch the blood. She whispered back and forth with Papa, words too low for Ines to take in fully.

"...kinder to die. She cannot--"

"Non! You will never..."

"How soon?"

"I cannot say."

"The bebe..."

New pains came and went, and Ines vaguely noted that they heralded her child's fight to escape the broken body sheltering her. She sobbed at the maid's sad eyes, at the silence as she wrapped the perfect but still and lifeless infant in a cloth, covering the thick blond curls, streaked with blood.

"The bebe?" Papa demanded.

Blanche shook her head slowly, tears in her eyes. She turned with a look of shock at a heavy sound behind her.

And, darkness returned.

Ines covered her face, sobbing at the image of the swaddled baby that remained with her.

"Do you understand now?" Jacque asked.

"What?" she shrieked. "That Papa has lost everything he loved? That he has been told it would be kinder to let me die? Do you think it comforts him to hear it? Would it comfort you?"

Jacque looked to her father, seemingly lost. "I do not understand. When Yvette was born dead..." He looked back to her, his eyes wide. "Could you see Pierre?"

"No. Blanche was between us, and... The baby..."

He cursed in a mixture of French and English, a vicious string of obscenity the likes of which she'd never heard from him. "All this time wasted! I would not have forced you to this had I known."

"Jacque?"

He didn't answer immediately, looking around the room frantically. "Do you trust me?"

"Yes. Of course." But her voice wavered at his question.

"Wish for a flower on the table."

"What?" What madness was this?

"Wish for it. Imagine that it is there and believe that it will be. Trust me in this."

Ines did as he asked, though she felt foolish doing it. A yellow rose in a blown-glass vase appeared next to her father.

Jacque sighed in relief. "Now wish for Blanche."

She tried...again...and again, but no one appeared.

"I told you this place is what you wanted it to be, but that does not include people who are not already of it."

Ines gasped and looked at her father in dawning understanding. "Papa?"

He smiled a wry smile. "You tell me I do too much. I am a foolish old man. I felt the pains when I pulled you from the snow but ignored the signs. I continued until the shock of the bebe..."

She bit her lip, speechless.

"So, you see... You suffer for no one. Jacque has passed on. I have passed on, and--"

Jacque looked up abruptly, and her father stopped speaking.

The implication wasn't lost on Ines. Her heart skipped in excitement. "Our daughter is here? The baby I hear crying?" Would she truly get to be a wife and mother as she'd dreamed?

Jacque smiled warmly. "She needs her mother, Ines."

She cupped his face and kissed him, vaguely noting her father taking his leave to give them privacy. And, it struck her.

Ines shook her head, dizzy, abruptly drained again. "I do not want to go back," she pleaded, her fingers grasping at Jacque's shirt weakly. She'd faced her memories and let go of the past. What more could be called for?

"Do not fear it," he soothed her. "You need only come again in the proper way. Then we will see our daughter."

She nodded, letting her eyes slip shut slowly.

"You have nothing to keep you there, Ines. Come home to me."

* * * *

Blanche rubbed her eyes, ignoring the latest of Doctor Wynn's protestations that she was a fool to believe a woman with such serious injuries, such fleeting periods of wakefulness, and no sign of physical response showed conscious thought.

She gasped as she glanced at Ines. The lady's eyes were open and trained on Blanche. Her finger's curled around Blanche's, as if confirming that she saw and understood.

"Doctor! She is awake!"

He turned back. "Now, you will see--"

He stopped and fell silent, as Ines smiled, a peaceful smile that made her look like an angel despite her sunken eyes and shorn hair.

Her voice was a mere whisper, audible only because the room was so still. "Nothing here--for me. I go--to the house--of my father." Her hand relaxed and her labored breathing tapered off.

The silence stretched between them.

"Such faith," Doctor Wynn offered in an awe-struck voice.

"They say Heaven is what you make of it," Blanche replied.

About the Author

Brenna Lyons wears many hats, sometimes all on the same day: former president of EPIC, author of more than 100 published works, owner of Fireborn Publishing, columnist, special needs teacher, wife, mother...and member in good standing of more than 60 writing advocacy groups.

In her first ten years published in novel-length, she's won 3 EPIC e-Book Awards (out of 15 finalists) and finaled for 3 PEARLS (including one Honorable Mention, second to NY Times Bestseller Angela Knight), 2 CAPAS, and a Dream Realm Award. She's also taken Spinetingler's Book of the Year for 2007.

Brenna writes in 26 established worlds plus stand-alones, poetry, articles and essays. She's a bestseller in indie/e fantasy and horror, straight genre and cross-genres thereof. Brenna has been termed "one of the most deviant erotic minds in the publishing world...not for the weak." (Rachelle for Fallen Angels Reviews) Milieu-heavy dark work is practically Brenna's calling card, with or without the erotic content.

She teaches classes in everything from POV studies to advanced editing, networking to marketing. Brenna enjoys hearing from people who read her work and can be reached by e-mail.

Website: http://www.brennalyons.com/

Facebook: http://www.facebook.com/brenna.lyons

Email: brennalyons4168@live.com

Also by this Author

Max Sec

URBAN GRIMM
Catch Me, If You Can
Three Wishes
Temptation of Eve

With Great Power
Undead in Blue
Evil Overlords Union Issue #1 Anthology
Undead Embrace
"Playing Games" in *Forbidden Love: Bad Boys*
"Marked" in *Forbidden Love: Wicked Women*
"The Master's Lover" in *Forbidden Love: Sacred Bands*

Available from **Logical Lust**

"Mine for the Night" in *The Cougar Book* Anthology

Available from **Coming Together Charity Anthologies**

INSTINCT SERIES
"Foundling" in *Coming Together: Into the Light* Anthology

"Claim Mate" (available separately and as part of the *Coming Together: Against the Odds* Anthology)
"The Fire God's Woman" in *Coming Together: Under Fire* Anthology

Available **self-published**

KEGIN SERIES
Earth-Born Lord
Graham: Training the Earth-Born Lord

NIGHT WARRIORS
Claiming a Lady

Stone Lord
Mother's Son

COLOR OF LOVE
A Safe Heart

Snapshots from a Poet's Life

Award-Winning Books

EPPIE/EPIC eBOOK AWARDS WINNERS
Coming Together: Against the Odds- 2010
Time Currents- 2010
Coming Together: Into the Light- 2011

EPPIE/EPIC eBOOK AWARDS FINALISTS
Fion's Daughter- 2004
Collected Poems: Book One- 2005 (now titled *Snapshots of a Poet's Life*)
Renegade's Run- 2005
Rites of Mating- 2006
All I Want for Christmas- 2006
Phaze in Verse- 2008
"The Fire God's Woman" in Coming Together: Under Fire- 2009
Three Wishes- 2010
Matchmaker's Misery- 2010
The Cougar Book- 2011
The Master's Lover- 2011
Bride Ball- 2011

DREAM REALM AWARDS FINALIST
Last Chance for Love- 2003

PEARL HONORABLE MENTION
Night Warriors- 2004

PEARL FINALISTS
Schente Night- 2003 (now included in *The Last of Fion's Daughters*)
König Cursebreakers- 2004 (now titled *Will of the Stone*)

JOYFULLY REVIEWED BEST BOOKS OF 2010
Written in the Stars- 2010

SPINETINGLER'S BOOK OF THE YEAR 2007

NOBODY: An Anthology of Dark Fiction- 2007 (Brenna's pieces of the anthology can be found in *Beyond the Veil*)

TRS's CAPA FINALISTS
Ultimate Warriors- 2004 (Brenna's portion is now available as *With Great Power*)
Written in the Stars

LOVE ROMANCE AND MORE CAFÉ BOOK OF THE YEAR RUNNER UP
Last Chance for Love- 2008

ROAD TO ROMANCE REVIEWERS' CHOICE AWARD
Prophecy: Revelations- 2004

LOVE ROMANCES REVIEWERS' CHOICE AWARD
Black Sail- 2003

ROMANCE JUNKIES BOOK CLUB STAFF PICK
TYGERS- 2003

FALLEN ANGELS ROMANCE RECOMMENDED READ
Devon's Price-2005 (now available in *Bearing Armen*)

JOYFULLY RECOMMENDED READ
Fairy Dreams- 2008
The Last of Fion's Daughters- 2009

TREBLE HEART FINALIST
Prophecy: Revelations- 2003